MARGARET... DAISY... DALE...

From the surf of Maine to lakeshore Milwaukee to Canada's Pacific mists, each of the Wallace women—a mother and her two daughters—is looking across her treasured home waters to the horizons of change...

These three women—warm, funny and courageous—are about to ride a bittersweet merry-go-round of joy and pain, love and illusion, reconciliation and rediscovery, in this classic bestseller that has won the hearts of women everywhere.

*Three Women
at the Water's
Edge*

A NOVEL BY NANCY THAYER

"COMPELLING, ABSORBING AND RICH."
—Publishers Weekly

THREE WOMEN AT THE WATER'S EDGE
Nancy Thayer
_____ 96064-6 $6.99 U.S./$7.99 CAN.

Publishers Book and Audio Mailing Service
P.O. Box 070059, Staten Island, NY 10307
Please send me the book(s) I have checked above. I am enclosing $_____ (please add $1.50 for the first book, and $.50 for each additional book to cover postage and handling. Send check or money order only—no CODs) or charge my VISA, MASTERCARD, DISCOVER or AMERICAN EXPRESS card.

Card Number_____

Expiration date_____Signature_____

Name_____

Address_____

City_____State/Zip_____
Please allow six weeks for delivery. Prices subject to change without notice. Payment in U.S. funds only. New York residents add applicable sales tax.   TWWE 10/96

TODAY JOANNA HAS THE LIFE SHE'D ALWAYS DREAMED OF...

Joanna Jones, the successful host of *Fabulous Homes*, a New York-based TV show, seems to have it all. Blessed with great looks, she has a successful lover and a job that gives her fame and money, while allowing her to indulge her passion for beautiful homes.

TOMORROW SHE MIGHT LOSE IT ALL...

Suddenly and shockingly, Joanna will discover what she doesn't have: a committed relationship she can depend on. Now she faces a stunning discovery alone and makes the tough decision to leave her glittering life for an old Nantucket house on the ocean, new friends, and unexpected enemies. The choices ahead will test her courage; the surprising twists of fate will challenge her faith as she faces a day of ashes, a time of sorrow, and one extraordinary new chance for love, happiness and....

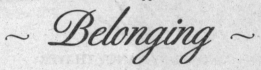

~ *Belonging* ~

BY NANCY THAYER

"Nancy Thayer has a rare talent for conveying the complexity and richness of women."
—*Publishers Weekly*

GREAT EXPECTATIONS

GR**e**AT
EXPECTATIONS

NOVELIZATION BY *Deborah Chiel*
BASED ON THE NOVEL BY *Charles Dickens*
BASED ON THE MOTION PICTURE WRITTEN BY
Mitch Glazer

St. Martin's Paperbacks

GREAT EXPECTATIONS

Copyright © 1998 by Twentieth Century Fox Film Corporation. All rights reserved.

Cover photograph copyright © 1998 by Twentieth Century Fox Film Corporation. All rights reserved.

All rights reserved. No part of this book may be used or reproduced in any manner whatsoever without written permission except in the case of brief quotations embodied in critical articles or reviews. For information address St. Martin's Press, 175 Fifth Avenue, New York, N.Y. 10010.

ISBN: 0-312-96303-3

Printed in the United States of America

St. Martin's Paperbacks edition/January 1998

St. Martin's Paperbacks are published by St. Martin's Press, 175 Fifth Avenue, New York, NY 10010.

10 9 8 7 6 5 4 3 2 1

For Gary Shapiro

CHAPTER 1

It should have been the happiest night of his life—a night for champagne and caviar, for laughter and celebration, for dancing and staying up until dawn and making love with the only woman he had ever loved. Jimmy Bell should have been giddy with joy, looking forward to the future, flushed with the kind of triumph that few people his age could even hope to achieve.

The New York City night was cold, with a sharp wind blowing along the empty, rotting piers that jutted out over the East River. A light dusting of snow had fallen earlier, and the bitter taste of winter was in the air. But the falling temperature shouldn't have made a difference to someone who so recently had been wrapped in the warm mantle of freshly minted success, surrounded by new friends and admirers eager to toast his talents and accomplishments.

The tantalizing possibility of a night such as this was what lured young men and women from small towns in Alabama and Iowa, New Hampshire and South Dakota, drew them to New York City like iron filings to a magnet. They dreamed all their lives of the chance to bask in the spotlight, to greet the next sunrise knowing that their name was on the lips of those who mattered most in the city. They dreamed of fame, of adoring fans, of applause and acclamation.

But not Jimmy Bell. He had never aspired to be a celebrity. He had never imagined himself living in New York, being cheered by the critics, praised by people whose approval gave him entree to the most exclusive addresses. He hadn't even dared to believe that his talent was worthy of recognition. It wasn't that he lacked for a dream. For more than half of his twenty-eight years, Jimmy had carried in his heart a shining image, a vision of perfection. Her name was Estella. He yearned for her with every breath and heartbeat.

He could see her face now as he stared down at the river, smooth and black as satin, empty of boat traffic in the predawn hours. The sky was black except for a sliver of pale moon that shone weakly through the layer of clouds that had brought the snow. Somewhere on the highway behind him an ambulance's siren shrieked as it raced through the darkness. Otherwise, he was surrounded by silence. He took a swig from the bottle of rum in his hand, noticed it was empty, unceremoniously tossed it over the railing that separated him from the river. The bottle landed with a muted splash.

Jimmy shivered as he watched the bottle skip across the water before it sank out of view. He'd grown up around water, had learned to swim almost before he could walk, to fish before he could read. He'd driven a boat years before he'd earned his driver's license. But the cold, polluted river that swirled below him was as unfamiliar and forbidding as the city itself had been when he'd first arrived.

He stuck his hand in the pocket of his leather jacket and found what he was looking for, an unopened pint of rum. He twisted off the cap, took a long gulp, and closed his eyes, hoping to blot out all memory of the evening just passed. The alcohol slipped easily down his throat and produced a momentary glow in his belly but otherwise failed to produce the effect he'd been seeking. He needed to make his feelings go away. He was searching for oblivion.

There wasn't much that frightened Jimmy Bell. He had too little to lose, even now, with the riches of the city glittering within his reach. Especially now, after all the hurtful things he'd said and done tonight. So he paid no attention to the footsteps coming up behind him, barely flinched when he felt cold, hard steel pressed against the back of his head.

"Don't move," a voice whispered hoarsely.

Jimmy smiled. Somewhere in his rum-soaked mind he registered the awareness that he could be in danger, that someone might be pointing a gun at him. But he didn't really care. The threat of trouble was a welcome diversion from his more immediate concerns.

When he opened his eyes, a pimply-faced Latino kid was glaring at him, and a gun was poking into his stomach. "What's so funny?" the kid demanded.

Life. The crazy way things turned out. The fact that he was getting mugged, which was no less than he deserved. "Nothing," he said. Anticipating the inevitable, he handed the kid his wallet. "Here."

The boy, who looked more scared than tough, gawked as he extracted the wad of cash that Jimmy had earlier withdrawn from the ATM.

"My watch?" asked Jimmy.

The kid stared at Jimmy, as if trying to decide whether he was smart or crazy.

"Sure," he said nervously. "Why not?"

Jimmy removed his watch and handed it over. It was new and expensive, a gift to himself on a day not too long ago when he'd begun to believe the stories people were telling about him. He wanted to believe them, to trust in his good fortune. But trust didn't come easy, and the greater part of his brain still didn't accept that he deserved what providence had chosen to bestow on him.

"Drink?" he offered the kid.

The boy jabbed his gun deeper into Jimmy's belly. "You blind?" he demanded.

Jimmy shrugged. He was just trying to be friendly. The kid was wearing a threadbare ski jacket. He looked cold and miserable, and a shot of rum was probably exactly what he needed. It sure was doing him a world of good. But, hey, he thought, no use forcing the guy to have a good time.

"More for me," he said.

He helped himself to another generous swig, which seemed to anger the kid, because he pointed the gun at Jimmy's face and cocked the hammer.

Jimmy felt as if he were in a movie, starring in the role of the tough guy who didn't give a shit, usually played by Bruce Willis or Clint Eastwood. He stuck his index finger in the barrel of the gun. *Go ahead,* he silently dared the skinny little punk, whose eyes looked as if they were about to bug out of his head. *Make my day.*

"Hey! Whatta you doin'?" the kid screamed.

"Crime prevention." Jimmy grinned. He

was finally enjoying himself. In fact, this was the most fun he'd had in weeks.

The kid swung the gun from side to side, trying to extricate Jimmy's finger from the barrel. "I'll blow your hand off! Get it out!"

"Nope. Not until you have a drink with me." Jimmy hated drinking alone, and that's all he'd been doing for hours now. Pouring booze down his throat, working hard at getting drunk. The kid reminded him of who he could have been, had his life taken just a slightly different turn. Angry and scared and desperate enough to do something stupid.

"Fuck you," the kid said, batting away the bottle of rum.

The kid's anger kindled his own rage. Jimmy took a chance and slammed the bottle against the kid's forehead. His sneak attack succeeded. The kid dropped the gun and clutched his head. "Awrgh! *Conio!*" he moaned.

Jimmy almost laughed out loud. He wondered whether this was the punk's first time out trying to rob someone. He thought about asking, then realized he didn't give a shit. Mugged by a fuckin' amateur, a guy who was such an incompetent that Jimmy had to teach him the goddamn A-B-C's. A great New York story . . . if only he had someone to tell it to.

He freed his finger from the gun barrel and pointed the gun at the kid's heart. He wasn't planning to pull the trigger—he wasn't that far gone. But he wanted the kid to get a taste of his own medicine, maybe make him think twice before he tried this crap again. He held up the rum, wordlessly inviting the kid to take a sip.

"Jesus Christ," the kid mumbled. "Fine. Let's drink."

Jimmy smiled. Once, a long time ago in what now seemed like another life, a man had scared him half to death. He still remembered how his terror had made everything look different and unfamiliar. Afterwards, when the threat had passed, the sky and sun had lost their garish Technicolor, and the world around him had regained its normal size and shape. But he could never forget the sense of knowing with absolute certainty that if he said or did the wrong thing, he would be killed. Though at the time he wouldn't have guessed it, the incident had proved to be a useful memory, a touchstone that had seen him through many difficult moments. And never more so than now.

Still aiming the gun where it would do the most harm, he handed the kid the bottle.

"I got a goddamn headache," the boy whined.

"The rum'll help," said Jimmy, his own head beginning to hurt now. The boy guzzled down a healthy dose of rum, more than Jimmy was happy to see disappear.

"I'd like my wallet back," he said.

The kid stashed the bottle in his jacket pocket and handed over the wallet.

Jimmy checked the billfold. As he'd suspected, it was empty. "My cash," he said.

The kid forked over the money.

"Watch," said Jimmy. Maybe he should switch careers, keep the gun, reinvent himself as a holdup artist. "That gold necklace you're wearing," he said, getting into the part.

"What?" The kid scowled. "Hey, kiss my ass!"

Jimmy shoved the gun barrel against the kid's forehead. Now that the tables were turned, he wanted him to experience firsthand the particular sensation of a loaded gun pressed against flesh.

"It says 'Rafael' on it," the kid said sullenly.

Jimmy pushed the gun harder against his temple. The kid would have a red mark there in the morning, a souvenir to remember him by.

The kid's hands shook as he pulled the necklace over his head and gave it Jimmy. "What the hell you gonna do with it?"

Jimmy examined the necklace in the dim light of the street lamp that shone overhead. The name was spelled out in large, ornate letters; the chain felt heavy as he slipped it around his neck. He figured it was real gold, probably cost as much as he used to make in a week. "You Rafael?"

"Why the hell else would I be wearing that?"

A good question. Rafael obviously wasn't the kind of guy who had the urge to shed his past and take on somebody else's identity. Jimmy, on the other hand, was becoming an expert in hating himself so much that changing places with an undernourished, bumbling, would-be mugger had its appeal. Maybe he should keep the necklace, leave town, and start over somewhere else as Rafael. He couldn't think of anyone who would miss him, certainly not in New York, probably not back home either. He'd always been pretty much of a loner, never made too many friends, not even as a kid.

"I'm Jimmy Bell," he said, wishing he knew who Jimmy Bell really was.

Rafael wasn't the only one with a headache. Jimmy's head was beginning to pound, and the pain was going to get worse. It would take a lot more than a couple of aspirins to cure the hangover that he had coming to him. He could already feel the alcohol loosening its grip on his brain; he was getting sober too fast, way before he was ready to face the world without the numbing effects of liquor to soften the edges. He motioned to Rafael to pass over the rum and guzzled down enough to postpone the prospect of sobriety.

"Sometimes," he said, as the booze began working its way into his bloodstream, "don't you wonder how different your life would have been if just one thing, one little thing, hadn't happened?"

Rafael glared at him. "All the damn time," he muttered, rubbing his cheekbone where Jimmy had hit him with the bottle.

The lights of the city, reflected in the water, danced along the top of the river. The effect was magical, as long as he didn't stop to consider what lay beneath the surface. Too late now, he recalled an important lesson that he'd learned as a child: that appearances could be deceiving, and deception led to heartbreak.

"Pull one thread, and the whole thing comes apart," he said softly.

His past and present had collided tonight. All his hopes for the future seemed destined to go unmet. How dared he to expect anything more than what destiny had decreed to be his fate?

CHAPTER 2

Dusk was falling. The fishermen of DeSoto Bay on Florida's west coast had hauled in their nets and gone home for dinner, and boat traffic was light. The water was calm, the gently lapping waves tipped with silver by the setting sun. Bands of red and pink and violet were splashed across the sky all the way to the Gulf of Mexico, streaks of pastel watercolors on a pale blue canvas.

Dusk was Jimmy Bell's favorite time of day. As he so often did in the late afternoon, Jimmy was puttering around the tiny inlet in the battered skiff that he'd inherited from his Uncle Joe. The bay was dotted with a series of uninhabited islands, and Jimmy was headed for the one that he had come to think of as his own.

His plan was to buy it some day, as soon as

he was all grown up and rich. He would live there by himself, in the house that he would build with the help of Uncle Joe, and he would watch the sunset every day from his porch. He would fish and paint beautiful pictures that he'd hang up on the wall, and he'd only allow the people he liked to step foot on his land, which most certainly did not include his Aunt Maggie.

Jimmy cut the engine and beached the skiff, jumping out in his bare feet to tie the boat up to a rusty bar that jutted out over the water. He frowned as he noticed a partially deflated raft that lay a few yards away from where he stood. Footprints in the damp sand told him that someone else had recently landed on his island.

The intruder, whoever he was, was nowhere to be seen. Perhaps he was fishing on the far end of the island, or maybe he'd been picked up by a passing boat. Jimmy turned his back on the raft, pulled his book bag out of the skiff, and strolled down the beach to where earlier in the week he'd spotted a barracuda cavorting in the slight depression formed by a sandbar.

The air was still, except for a faint breeze that ruffled Jimmy's hair, which was bleached blond by the sun. The only sounds to be heard were the gentle hiss of waves lapping against the sand, the occasional screech of a sea gull wheeling overhead. It was only here on the island that Jimmy found peace and solitude. At home, his aunt was always fighting with him or Uncle Joe, faulting them for one thing or another no matter how hard they worked to please her. Aunt Maggie was very strict and not all that nice, and Jimmy couldn't understand why Uncle Joe put up with her. Jimmy didn't have a choice: he was just a kid, and ten-year-olds weren't allowed to live on their own, even if he could probably take better care of himself than Maggie, who was usually too stoned to pay much attention to him.

Things would be different if his parents were still alive. He had only a few memories of his mother and father, fragments of his life before the accident that he cherished so dearly he hesitated to recall them too often, for fear they might fade or begin to seem less real.

Aunt Maggie loved to remind him how fortunate he was that she'd agreed to take him in. Otherwise, she said, he could have wound up a ward of the state, whatever that meant, or in a foster home. "Your mother and I weren't close, growing up," she'd said time and again, "but blood is blood, so I figure I have to put up with you."

It comforted him to think that his mother hadn't been anything like her younger sister. He certainly didn't remember her inviting men into the house all the time, the way Aunt Maggie did. The kids in the neighborhood laughed at Maggie behind her back and called her a

whore. *Do you know about the men?* he wanted
to ask Uncle Joe. *And don't you care?* But he
kept the questions to himself, because he didn't
want to make his uncle feel worse than he
probably already did.

He stood quietly and gazed into the shallows, willing the silver-fleshed barracuda to
appear. When the fish swam into view he
smiled. All that day, as his teacher had droned
on, he had thought about this moment. Now he
squatted in the sand and pulled out his drawing
pad and pen. He began sketching the barracuda, trying to replicate its long, slender shape
and sharp fins.

He knew he was good at drawing, the best
in his class, and he enjoyed doing it more than
just about anything else, except fishing with
Uncle Joe. Aunt Maggie thought that drawing
was a waste of time. "Can't make a living that
way. Go do something useful," she'd scold
him when she caught him with his sketchpad.

But he almost couldn't stop himself. His fingers would sometimes twitch with impatience
to grab a pencil and start drawing. Occasionally, he was even pleased with the results. He
liked what he was doing now, how real the
barracuda looked as he filled in the lines and
shadows. He would have been happy to stay
until nightfall sketching his subject. But the
'cuda must have spotted its dinner, because
suddenly it flashed through the water and dis-

appeared beneath the nearby rickety dock that someone had abandoned many years earlier.

Taking care to avoid the rusted nails and splinters that protruded from the weathered boards, Jimmy walked out to the end of the dock. He lay down on his stomach with his head hanging out over the dock, his face only a few inches above the water. He peered down, hoping to catch a glimpse of the 'cuda feasting on its prey, but all he saw was his own face reflected back at him. When his eyes adjusted to the murky light beneath the surface, he gasped in surprise. He thought maybe he was hallucinating, because he could have sworn he saw a man's face hovering just beneath the water! The man's eyes were wide open, and his mouth was creased in a grin.

A second later, an arm shot up through the water and grabbed him by the throat. Jimmy felt himself being hauled off the dock to land kicking and screaming in the waist-deep water. Struggling to break free of the hand around his neck, he blinked the water out of his eyes and saw that the face and arm belonged to a dark-haired man dressed in a torn orange jumpsuit. The words PROPERTY OF FLORIDA STATE PENITENTIARY were written in big, bold letters across the front.

Jimmy thought of the raft he'd seen earlier on the beach, and the set of footprints in the sand. The man must have escaped from the penitentiary.

"Please!" he cried, as the convict picked him up by the neck. "Don't! I—"

"Shut up!" the convict snarled. He hobbled out of the water, his feet bound together by steel shackles, and threw Jimmy onto the dock. Though he was a big man, the effort seemed to have cost him some pain, because he clutched at the bloody gash on his left side and groaned loudly. His large hand clenched tightly around Jimmy's arm, he pulled himself up onto the dock and massaged the part of his legs that had been rubbed raw from the shackles.

"What's your name?" the convict demanded.

Seated only inches away from a real live escaped con, Jimmy was torn between terror and fascination. "Jimmy Bell," he stammered.

"Where do you live?"

The man was fierce-looking, with brown eyes that flashed angrily at him and insisted he tell the truth. "Cortez," Jimmy said. "A block from the pier. My Uncle Joe's a—"

"He has tools?" he broke in impatiently.

"Sure, sure." Jimmy nodded, his arm hurting where the convict's fingers were digging into his flesh. "He's got lawn mowers and—"

The convict interrupted him again. "Do you know what bolt cutters are?"

Jimmy imagined his uncle's tool kit. "I think."

"Do you know what food is?"

"Food?" Jimmy stared at the convict, trying to figure out whether the man was joking. He was ten years old, not a little kid.

But the man wasn't smiling, in fact, quite the opposite. He leaned toward Jimmy, close enough that Jimmy could feel the man's breath on his face. He had flecks of foam in the corners of his mouth, like a rabid dog, and the look in his eyes reminded Jimmy of a treed coon.

"I know your name," the man said in a low voice that made Jimmy shiver in spite of the heat of the day. "I know where you live. I can find you and gut you like a fish. I'll pull out your insides and make you eat 'em. You hear me, boy?"

Jimmy's heart was thudding so hard that he almost couldn't draw a breath. There weren't too many places to hide in Cortez, and he'd stupidly told the convict enough about himself that he could easily find him. He believed the convict's threats. He looked like the kind of person who would slit a man's—or a boy's— throat without thinking twice about it.

"Be here tomorrow morning, dawn, with the cutters and food or I'll kill you for sure. Understand?" the convict growled.

Jimmy nodded. His mouth felt parched with fear.

"Tell anyone, your folks—"

"They're dead," Jimmy whispered hoarsely.

"Tell anyone, and the last sound you hear will be your own scream."

Jimmy gulped. How could this be happening to him, here, on his island? An escaped convict was something you read about in books or watched on TV. But this was no made-up story. This convict was real, and he had the prison uniform and the cut in his side to prove it. Jimmy wondered how he'd been wounded, whether he'd been hurt by another prisoner or one of the guards when he'd been making his getaway. And where had he found that raft? Jimmy wished he had the guts to ask the convict how he'd escaped. But he didn't dare. He was sure the convict meant what he said. One false move, and he would be dead, just like his parents.

The convict let go of his arm. "Go!" he ordered.

Jimmy didn't stop to ask any questions. He grabbed his book bag, willed his legs to move, and raced down the length of the dock, ignoring the splinters. He stumbled and tripped over his feet when he hit the sand. He was moving so fast that it wasn't until he jumped into his skiff and cast off that he realized he'd left his sketchbook behind on the dock. And because he was too scared to take a backwards glance, he missed seeing the convict, his face contorted in pain from his wound, studying his drawing of the barracuda.

The sky was more purple than blue by the time Jimmy reached the Cortez dock and pulled into the slip next to his uncle's fishing boat. The plaintive, bittersweet sound of Miles Davis's "Sketches of Spain" drifted through the window of the boat, which meant that Joe must still be aboard, cleaning fish or taking care of one of the many chores that came with running a charter fishing service. Jimmy wasn't ready to face him yet, not when he was still feeling so shaky and scared. Uncle Joe knew him better than anyone else. He was afraid that his uncle would read his expression, figure that something was up, and try to get him to admit what was going on.

He might have cleared the dock without being seen if he hadn't slipped and banged his shin against the pier. He couldn't stop himself from crying out, which brought Uncle Joe out onto the deck of his boat.

He greeted Jimmy with the nickname he'd given him when he was a toddler. "Whoa, Chub-chub."

"Uncle Joe, hey." Jimmy smiled up at his uncle. Joe's face was tinted dark brown by the sun, and he had ropey muscles from spending most of his thirty-five years hauling fishing nets, mowing lawns, and working at any other jobs that came his way. "So you went out today?"

"Hell, yeah," said Joe. He lit a cigarette and stuck it in his mouth. Then he unwound the water hose that was curled in a corner and started washing salt off the deck. The boat needed a paint job, but Joe couldn't afford the paint or the time, so he compromised by keeping the decks as clean as possible. "Got a nice tan. No fish, of course. Tino's put out traps. Goin' for those bugs like everybody else. Lobsters. Ah, what the hell. It all swims." He grimaced, thinking of the lobsters, which he hated to catch, much less eat. "Or crawls."

Eager to get home before Joe so he could find and stash the bolt cutter in his book bag, Jimmy managed a weak smile, then turned to go. Joe looked surprised. Normally, Jimmy hung around the boat with Joe, partly because he enjoyed his company, but also because he preferred to help him with the chores rather than face his aunt alone.

"J. B., where's the fire?" asked Joe.

"Nothing. Homework."

"Okay." He hesitated as he tossed his cigarette into the bay. Then he said, "Listen, Maggie's kind of on a rant. Be careful, okay?"

Jimmy gnawed at his thumbnail. Uncle Joe never made much of Aunt Maggie's moods unless things got really bad. He wasn't sure which worried him more: the convict's threats, or Aunt Maggie on a rant. "You comin' home soon?"

" 'Bout an hour. Get your work done, we'll go to Carvel," Joe promised. "Oh yeah, we got us a gardening job, so rest those muscles."

"Great," Jimmy said. They needed the money. The fish hadn't been biting much lately, and the charter business was slow. Aunt Maggie was always carrying on about how broke they were, complaining that Joe was a no-good bum who couldn't make a buck if it were free for the taking. But Uncle Joe was anything but lazy. The problem was that the work was hard to come by.

He glanced out at the bay and had a sudden urge to tell Uncle Joe everything—about the convict and his threats and what he had promised to do for the man. "Joe?" he said.

"Yeah?"

He changed his mind just as suddenly. *I know where you live,* the convict had said. He might not stop at killing Jimmy. He might go after Uncle Joe and Aunt Maggie, too. "Nothin'."

"Hey, James," said Joe, as if he sensed that Jimmy was concerned about something and wanted to cheer him up. "How do ya smoke a swordfish?"

It was their special private joke, and it never

failed to make Jimmy grin. "Put the bill in your mouth and light the tail," he said and immediately felt better.

He was still smiling as Joe sent him off with a wink and a wave. He jogged away from the dock, past the rotting, beached fishing boats that lay lined up like corpses on the sand. He passed a row of unkempt shacks that should have been condemned long ago and turned down the road to his house. Cortez was a sad little town, a place to get away from if only you had somewhere else to go. There was no right or wrong side of the tracks in Cortez. Every street was rundown, every building a candidate for urban renewal. Even the park looked depressing, with the trees all badly in need of pruning and a playground full of rusted equipment. The kiddie pool was cracked and had been declared too dangerous to use, and the sprinkler was broken and had been taken out of service.

The teenagers, with nowhere else to meet, had chased away the younger kids and claimed the playground as their territory. They came with their boom boxes to drink beer and smoke dope and play the heavy metal music their parents wouldn't tolerate. Jimmy normally gave the park a wide berth, especially when the Rhinebold twins were there. The Rhinebolds, who lived across the street from Jimmy, were fifteen, blonde, and very pretty. Jimmy had a crush on Gloria, but most of the time he was too shy even to say hello to her.

The two of them were hanging out now on the swings, the short skirts billowing in the wind. He glanced sideways and tried to catch a glimpse of their underwear before they spotted him. But Gloria saw him first and shouted, "Jimmy! Jimmy, c'mere!"

"Gimme a push, Jimmy!" her sister Diane chimed in.

Jimmy ignored them both and ran faster. He could hear them yelling all the way to First Street, where he turned left and kept jogging until he reached the shabby two-story apartment building where he lived. He darted up the stairs, then stopped to catch his breath before he shoved open the door and tiptoed into the apartment. The television was on and tuned to "Jeopardy," but the living room was empty. Someone—Joe, most likely—had cleaned up the papers and empty bottles that were usually strewn about.

Before he had a chance to sneak into his room unseen, the door to his aunt and uncle's bedroom opened, and a stocky man walked out. His face was red and sweaty, as if he'd just been working hard at something, and he was tucking his shirt into his pants when he noticed Jimmy. The man, whom Jimmy didn't recognize as one of Maggie's regular visitors, hesitated a moment, and Jimmy guessed that he was trying to decide whether or not to say hello. Instead, he quickly crossed the room, tousled Jimmy's hair as he passed by, and left the apartment without speaking to him.

Maybe now Aunt Maggie would lighten up. She usually did after a visit from one of her "friends," as Jimmy thought of them. He wondered whether the men gave her money, whether she treated them the way she treated Uncle Joe. He bet not, because then they wouldn't keep coming around. It was different with Uncle Joe. He was her husband, so he had no choice but to love her and put up with her bad temper.

He walked past her bedroom on the way to his own, figuring that if she were going to tear into him, he may as well show his face and have her get it over with. Maggie was sitting cross-legged on the bed. The sheets were rumpled, as if she had just gotten up, and she was dressed only in a tank top and panties. Jimmy had overheard a couple of the older boys talking about Aunt Maggie. She was sexy, they said, for a thirty-year-old. His mother had been beautiful, with long brown hair and dark brown eyes. Aunt Maggie looked nothing like her sister. Jimmy wasn't sure what sexy was supposed to look like, but he didn't think Aunt Maggie was it.

She had her stash of pot in front of her and was busy sorting through it, separating the seeds and the stems. Soon the apartment would smell of the stuff, and Aunt Maggie would laugh at whatever Uncle Joe said to her. Right now she was too busy to do more than briefly glance up at Jimmy before she went back to rolling a joint. She would probably ignore him for the rest of the evening, which was just fine, because he had enough to worry about tonight without having to answer any of her nasty questions.

He was too nervous to do his homework, and what the hell? He might not be alive on Monday to hand it in. Waiting for Uncle Joe to get home, he lay on his bed and tried not to think about the convict. But no matter what pictures he conjured up to distract himself, his thoughts kept coming back to the same image. Even when he closed his eyes, he saw the convict as clearly as if he were standing right there in front of him: the man's dark brown eyes boring into his, his face creased in pain, the blood-stained wound in his side, the shackles that bound his legs.

He rubbed his throat where the convict had grabbed him, and wondered where the man was now, whether he had hobbled back to the raft to try and sleep, or whether he was still sitting on the dock, waiting for the night to pass and for Jimmy to reappear. And when was the last time he'd had something to eat? Jimmy tried to imagine himself alone and hungry and cold. He wished he knew what crime the convict had committed that he'd been sent to the penitentiary. Perhaps he'd needed money for his family and had robbed a bank. Or maybe he'd gotten into a fight and beaten someone up. Or maybe he'd murdered someone. . . .

The convict was on his mind all through dinner. He pushed his fork around his plate and could barely choke down a bite of food, but his lack of appetite escaped his aunt and uncle's attention. The ice cream cone that Uncle Joe bought him for dessert gave him no pleasure, even though Uncle Joe sprang for chocolate sprinkles, Jimmy's favorite. He was certain that he would never fall asleep, but he turned out the light and huddled under the covers, listening to the rain that had just begun to fall.

A peal of thunder made him sit up in bed in time to see a lightning bolt flash across the sky. The convict was crouched in the corner, holding a knife. "I told you I know where you live," he said. "Are you ready to die?"

"No!" Jimmy screamed, and shocked himself awake. He was curled up in a ball, whimpering with fright, but he was alone in the room. The rain was beating against the half-open window, and the sky was alive with the crackle of lightning. His covers lay on the floor in a heap, and his hands shook as he reached down to retrieve them.

The alarm clock said 3:12. It would be light out in just a few hours. Wide awake now, he jumped out of bed and got dressed in a hurry. The apartment was quiet, and he had work to do.

His first stop was the bathroom. The convict hadn't said anything about medicine, but he was hurt and probably needed some pills. Jimmy opened the medicine cabinet and peered inside, trying to decipher the labels on the vials that were lined up haphazardly on the shelves. Most of them belonged to Aunt Maggie, who was always complaining of one sort of pain or another. Jimmy grabbed a few at random, as well as a fistful of bandages. He eyed the rubbing alcohol, cough syrup, and suntan lotion, but decided to stick to the basics. He would have plenty to carry as it was.

Next he headed for the kitchen. Food, the convict had said, but he hadn't mentioned what kind. Not that there was much to choose from in the refrigerator or cupboards. Aunt Maggie wasn't big on shopping, and Uncle Joe was usually too busy. Jimmy thought about what he would want to eat if he were shipwrecked on a desert island and hoped he was making the right choices. He threw his supplies into a garbage bag, then decided that the convict needed something to drink. There was a six-pack of orange soda in the refrigerator, but that belonged to Aunt Maggie and Jimmy wasn't supposed to drink it without her permission. Anyway, who ever heard of a convict drinking orange soda? He remembered the raft and the way the man had sprung out of the water to grab him. *Like a pirate,* he thought, and reached into the cupboard for the bottle of rum that one of Uncle Joe's customers had given him for Christmas.

The bolt cutters were in Uncle Joe's tool box. He tiptoed past his aunt and uncle's room on the way out. Their door was open, but they were fast asleep, tucked one against the other like a pair of spoons. Nevertheless, he held his breath until he was safely down the steps and outside the building. As long as no one spotted him rushing toward the dock, he was home free.

Though a hard rain continued to fall, the thunder had receded to a dull boom in the distance, and the lightning was only a pale glimmer against an invisible horizon. Jimmy could see almost nothing in the pitch-black darkness, but he'd navigated the bay so often that he could have found his way blindfolded to the island. As the skiff danced between the churning waves, shapes seemed to loom at him out of the storm. But the shapes failed to materialize into any recognizable form. Jimmy was alone on the water, haunted by the phantoms of his imagination.

After what seemed like an eternity, he finally reached the island. He cut the engine and coasted the skiff onto the empty beach. He stood still a moment, listening for the convict. But all he could hear was the howling wind, and the rain slapping against the surface of the water. Slinging the garbage bag over one shoulder, he waded through the shallows and peered through the gloom but could find no sign of the convict. He was getting ready to call out a hello when a hand clamped down on his shoulder and spun him around.

The convict loomed over him, looking wet and haggard. "You alone?"

Jimmy tried to form the word "yes," tried to nod his head, but he felt paralyzed with fear. He could neither speak nor move.

"You deaf?" the convict demanded.

"No," Jimmy managed to choke out.

"No, you're not deaf, or no, you're not alone?"

Jimmy stared dumbly at the man, trying to sort out the question.

"Forget it," the convict said disgustedly. He grabbed the garbage bag and dumped out its contents onto the sand. He fell to his knees, grabbing at the food like a hungry dog.

"What the fuck is this?" he asked, holding up a jar of chocolate syrup.

"Bosco," said Jimmy, proud of himself for thinking to bring it.

"And this?" The convict held up a white-bread sandwich that was missing a few bites.

"A fluffernutter. I had some of it for a snack yesterday." It had tasted great, and he'd been looking forward to finishing it today, but he'd figured that the convict needed it more than he did.

The convict pried apart the slices of bread and studied the filling. He glared at the sticky sweet combination of marshmallow and peanut butter but wolfed down the sandwich almost without stopping to chew. Next he started cramming Kraft Singles into his mouth, pulling the cellophane from his lips, then dove into the jar of pickles. He finished up with the Bosco, which he dug out of the jar with his hands, smearing his face with the syrup as he devoured it.

"It's okay?" asked Jimmy nervously.

"What?" said the convict, mid-swallow.

"The food?"

"It's disgusting. But it'll do."

"I brought you something to drink," said Jimmy.

The convict momentarily stopped inhaling the food. "Bring it over. You get the bolt cutters?"

"Yes, sir," Jimmy said and trotted over to the skiff.

"Let's see 'em."

Jimmy dragged the heavy cutters over to the

convict, clutching the rum in his free hand. The convict's mouth formed what almost could have been taken for a smile as he grabbed the rum and guzzled it down like water. After emptying most of the bottle in no more than two gulps, he sat down and began working the cutters against the chain that bound his ankles.

"Shit," he hissed through gritted teeth. The effort required to cut the shackles was putting pressure on his side, and a thick stream of blood spurted out of the open wound. He pulled down the top of his prison uniform and splashed rum onto the gash to sterilize it, then reapplied himself to the shackles.

Jimmy grimaced in sympathy. Suddenly, he remembered the pills he'd brought with him.

"Here." He fished in his pocket and handed one of the bottles to the convict. "I took this for you."

The convict read the label and scowled. "Birth control pills?"

Jimmy frowned, angry at himself for bringing something that was of no use to the convict. "Here. This, too," he said. He gave the man another bottle along with a fistful of Band-Aids.

The convict squinted at the label, and his face brightened. "Ah, now we're talkin'. Percodan. Yessir." He ripped open the bottle and tipped it to his mouth, swallowing several of the tablets. "Good boy."

He sighed deeply, as the alcohol began to work its way into his system, dulling the pain. A few seconds' more work with the cutters and he'd sliced through the steel around his ankles. Gingerly, he applied the Band-Aid to his wound. It took some doing, because his hands were none too steady, and the cut was long and deep, but he managed to cover a good part of it.

"You bite your nails," he said as he carefully patted the Band-Aid in place. "That's a bad habit. People'll tell you the eyes are the windows to the soul. Bullshit. The hands, that's the sign of a gentleman."

The convict was the first person who'd ever mentioned his nailbiting. Surprised that the man had noticed, Jimmy glanced at his nails and wondered what the convict had meant by "windows to the soul." Could anyone see into his soul? Could they know he'd stolen food and medicine on behalf of a criminal? He clenched his fists and resolved to stop biting his nails.

The rain had slowed to a drizzle. The convict stood up wearily. "Okay, let's go," he said.

"Go?" Jimmy gaped at him.

"Get in the boat."

Jimmy wanted to protest, to remind the convict that he'd followed orders, brought him everything he'd asked for. Now all he wanted was to go home and get back to his regular life. But because he was too scared to argue with the man, he trudged the few feet to the skiff and climbed inside.

Holding his side to protect it, the convict shoved the skiff into the water, then clambered aboard. He positioned himself in the bow, facing Jimmy. "Go ahead," he said. "Drive."

"Where?" Jimmy asked, dreading the answer.

"Mexico."

"What?" He couldn't go to Mexico. He was just a kid, and if he weren't home in a couple of hours, Uncle Joe would be crazy with worry. Besides, they had a job to do today, and they needed the money. "How?" he said, close to crying.

"What, where, how!" the convict rasped. "What're you, a reporter?"

"We don't . . . I mean, there's not enough gas, and I don't . . . that's across the Gulf. I've never—"

"Calm down, boy. We'll get gas. Then we'll head west. No rush. We'll make it."

Jimmy blinked back his tears. He thought about Uncle Joe and Aunt Maggie, wondered what they would make of his disappearance. Uncle Joe would miss him, maybe Aunt Maggie would, too. Would they call the police? Had he left behind any clues that might help him get found before he reached Mexico? He stared into the distance, the wind blowing hard against his face. He was a good sailor, but he wasn't sure he was up to the challenge. He was even less sure about the skiff.

The convict, it seemed, had no such doubts. He smiled confidently as he stretched out in the boat. As if he could read Jimmy's mind, he said, "Sure, we'll make it. I got Jimmy at the wheel."

The rain had picked up again, and heavy waves rolled across the open sea. Jimmy faced the skiff away from the island, away from all that was familiar to him. Swollen drops of water pelted the boat as it chugged against the current. Night was fading, and the sky was beginning to lighten from black to gray in the east.

Jimmy imagined the big map of the world that stood in the corner of his classroom: Cuba was just south of Florida; Mexico was all the way west across the Gulf. How long would it take to reach the coast, he wondered. Where could they stop for gas, and how did the convict plan to pay for it? Jimmy didn't have any money with him. He doubted that the convict did either. Was he planning to hold up a gas station?

The piercing blast of an airhorn, signalling the approach of another boat, jolted him out of his anxious thoughts.

The convict sat up quickly and strained to

see through the murk. "What?" he demanded.

Jimmy stared ahead. It took a few seconds before he saw the boat, which he recognized as bearing the insignia of the Metro-Dade Police. "Police boat," he said.

"Stop here," the convict said, his voice low and quiet.

Jimmy threw the skiff into neutral. Out of the corner of his eye, he watched the convict crawl to the back of the skiff and climb over the gunwale into the water. He grabbed hold of the propeller and used it to hold himself up as he floated out of sight of the police boat.

The boat bore down on them. Jimmy felt the convict's gaze fixed on him, peering into his soul.

"Ahoy there, son!" one of the cops shouted through his bullhorn. "Are you all right?"

Jimmy nodded, then realized the cop couldn't see him. "Uh-huh," he shouted back.

"Where are you headed?" yelled the cop.

"Uh, nowhere, sir." But why would he be headed nowhere in the middle of a rainstorm, in the middle of the night? "Just . . ." His voice trailed off as he groped for a plausible explanation.

"An old lady over on Cat Cay thought she saw a raft out here yesterday. A man on it . . ." The cop's voice boomed across the narrow distance between them. "He'd be wearing an orange prison suit. Seen anything like that?"

Jimmy looked at the officer and thought about everything Uncle Joe had taught him about choosing between right and wrong. He thought about being scared and lonely, about the convict's threat to kill him, about the pained expression on the convict's face when he'd poured the rum on his wound. He crossed his fingers behind his back and said, "Nope."

"Well, come aboard, we'll give you a lift," called the cop.

"Thanks, but—"

A thick length of rope hit the deck of the skiff. "Tie up and come aboard," the cop insisted. "We'll take you home."

Jimmy looked down into the water. The convict had disappeared from sight.

CHAPTER 3

He sneaked back into the house just before dawn. When Uncle Joe came into his room to wake him up, he was safely in bed, pretending to be asleep. He was glad it was Saturday and not a school day. He couldn't have concentrated on spelling and arithmetic and social studies when all he could think about was what had happened to the convict. Had he swum away to safety and freedom? Or had he drowned there in the cold, dark waters of the Bay?

He helped Uncle Joe load up the truck with the lawn mowers, leaf blowers, and the rest of the yard tools. Instead of sitting up front with Uncle Joe as he usually did, he made room for himself in the bed of the truck alongside the gardening equipment. All the way to Sarasota, he lay on his back, lost in a daydream about his adventures of the previous night. Dense, dark storm clouds floated above the banyan trees during the half-hour ride down the coast. Jimmy's thoughts were stuck on a single track: Where was the convict? Was he safe? Was he warm? Was he hungry? Would he return to the island in search of Jimmy?

He must have nodded off, because he was suddenly awakened as the truck jostled along an unpaved road. Jimmy sat up and stretched, then stared in amazement when Uncle Joe made a right turn between two enormous stone pillars. Perched atop the right pillar was a screech owl, also carved out of stone; a marble mouse was trapped in its beak, and the owl's talons were painted with bright red nail polish. The words PARADISO PERDUTO were carved in large block letters across the left pillar.

Jimmy's mouth fell open in amazement as Uncle Joe continued slowly along a narrow road that wound through the property. Uncle Joe had told him that the estate was set on fifteen acres, and the overgrown lawns stretched in every direction for as far as he could see. Jimmy felt as if he had been transported to a lost city, frozen in time. Enormous party tents, tattered and covered with moss from having been left standing for so long, stood at intervals amidst the tall grass. Gold chairs lay peeling and choked with vines next to overturned banquet tables, their legs rusted to the color of dried blood. Pieces of linen, silver, and crystal were strewn about, all but swallowed by the jungle-thick vegetation.

A very wealthy person must have given a party years earlier and forgotten to clean up the mess. Clouds of flies buzzed in the warm, still air. The place reeked of rot and neglect, nature as a damp, humid corpse.

The road ended in front of a mansion, a two-story, gargoyle-encrusted house that made Jimmy think of a haunted house at an amusement park he'd once visited. Eager to get a closer look, he hopped off the truck and walked around to join Uncle Joe.

"Okay. You mow. I'll trim the sprinklers," he said and winked at his uncle.

Uncle Joe shook his head, as if he couldn't quite believe what he was seeing. "Very funny. Jesus. The land that time forgot." A glint in the dirt caught his eye. He bent down and dug out a tarnished sterling-silver fork, encrusted with mud. The handle was inscribed with a delicately designed monogram: NDD.

"Nora Driggers Dinsmoor," Joe murmured.

"What?" said Jimmy.

"That's who owns this place."

"What happened?" Jimmy asked.

Joe shrugged. "Looks like somebody just gave up. Wait here. I'm gonna go and see what they want us to do."

"Is it all right if I look around?"

"No," Joe said sternly. "Stay put 'til I get back. I mean it. God knows what's in these weeds."

Jimmy nodded and obediently sat down at the base of a crumbling marble pedestal, while Joe trudged off through the thick underbrush toward the house. He glanced around, still stunned by the wreckage, then looked at his hand. A ladybug glittered like a jewel on his palm. A second later, it spread its wings and flew away.

"Do you always do what your daddy says?" A girl's voice floated through the air from somewhere behind him.

Startled, he jerked his head around and found himself being scrutinized by a blond-haired girl who looked to be his age. His first thought was that she was very beautiful, and that she was dressed in the prettiest dress he'd ever seen, fit for a princess to wear to a party. His second thought was that she must have been spying on him and Uncle Joe. He wondered where she'd been hiding and for how long.

"N-n-no," he stammered. "I don't know." He took a deep breath and recovered himself. "Usually. Anyhow, he's not my—"

"What's your name?" she interrupted, examining him from head to toe as if he were some very rare species of animal that she had laid eyes on for the first time.

He squirmed beneath her gaze. "Jimmy Bell."

"My name's Estella," she announced, making it sound as if he should already know that.

"That's a pretty name." The instant the words were out of his mouth he wanted to take them back. He'd never said anything so dumb in his whole life. But he'd never heard of a more beautiful name, and it suited her perfectly.

"I know," she said. She tapped her foot impatiently, as if she were waiting for him to continue the conversation.

She was the princess, he was her humble servant. He tried desperately to guess what would win her approval. The best he could come up with was, "Do you live—?"

"Are you a gardener?" She wrinkled her perfect nose, and he knew he'd failed to please her.

"Just for now. For the summer. I help my uncle."

Graceful as a ballerina, she bent one knee and plucked a forget-me-not out of the grass. She daintily inhaled its fragrance, then smiled at him. "You smell like horseshit," she said.

He felt his cheeks flame bright red with shame. Was she telling the truth or just teasing him? He resisted the urge to lift his shirt and sniff it.

"Shower before you come next time," she

commanded him. She twirled around on one foot and sauntered off in the direction of a bamboo grove.

Jimmy felt his mouth flapping open and closed like a caught fish gasping for air. Trying to think of a suitably snappy response to her gibe, he started after her. But before he could take more than a couple of steps, he heard Joe calling him. "Hey, J. B.!"

He turned around and saw his uncle walking toward him, shaking his head. "We're outta here," Joe said as he stuck his wallet in his back pocket. "She slipped me five hundred dollars under the door. 'Gas money,' she called it. Weirdest thing."

Jimmy turned to look for Estella, but she had slipped away into the brush and was no longer visible. He stared at the bamboo trees, holding his breath, hoping she might change her mind and reappear.

"What?" asked Joe, getting into the cab of the truck.

Jimmy tore his eyes away from the grove. "Nothing. Can I ride with you?" he asked. He opened the passenger-side door and started to climb in next to Joe.

"Sure. Just don't sit too close." Joe grinned at him. "You smell like fertilizer."

Jimmy bunched up the front of his shirt and took a deep whiff. Then he sniffed at his arms. "Really? I do? I smell?"

Joe didn't answer him, just threw back his head and laughed. Then he threw a light punch to Jimmy's shoulder, as if to say, *What the hell difference does it make?* and turned on the motor.

Jimmy immediately decided to take a shower the second he got home. As his uncle backed the truck out down the driveway, Jimmy craned his neck out the window and kept his eyes fixed on the point at which he'd caught his last glimpse of Estella. The thought that he would most likely never see her again struck him as one of the meanest and most unfair things that had happened in his whole entire life.

He sat brooding all the way back to Cortez, but Uncle Joe was in too good a mood to notice his nephew's silence. He had five hundred dollars in his pocket that he'd earned by doing nothing more strenuous than taking a drive on a pretty summer day. It was like winning the lottery, and what were the odds of that happening to someone like him? He couldn't wait to tell Maggie, who was always carping at him because money was so tight, and they couldn't afford to buy all the things a girl like her wanted and deserved.

The heck with the bills. They were going to celebrate with a steak dinner at one of the fancy restaurants in Bradenton, but not before Maggie went out and bought herself a sexy dress and some long, dangling earrings to match. He would buy the kid something special, too. A set of watercolor paints, like the one he was always staring at in the window of the art store, or some felt-tip markers. Or maybe, thought Joe, he'd splurge and get them both. Because how often did a guy get paid for doing nothing?

He couldn't get upstairs fast enough, and he was already talking as he burst into the apartment. "Mag, you're not gonna believe—"

She waved her hand at him to tell him to be quiet because she was on the phone, the receiver cradled on her shoulder, pacing the living room as she puffed nervously on a cigarette.

"Yes, well," she was saying, nodding her head enthusiastically. "That sounds . . . I'll be glad to. You got it. Three on Saturday. And thank you."

Joe vaguely registered the fact that his wife was speaking in a very un-Maggie-like voice, so polite and obliging that she could have been imitating a character out of one of the soap operas she watched most afternoons. But he was so preoccupied with his news that he pushed that thought aside and said, as soon as she hung up the phone, "We were at the weirdest place today. It was like a castle that—"

"That was Nora Driggers Dinsmoor," Maggie broke in. She crossed her arms on her chest and stared at Joe, as if expecting him to confess to some crime he didn't know he'd committed.

"What'd she want?" he asked nervously.

"Him!" Maggie squealed. She pointed a long red fingernail at Jimmy. "My little nephew! The richest lady in the county, maybe the goddamn state, wants my little guy to play with her niece."

She was smiling now as she threw an arm around Jimmy, who held his breath, waiting for what he knew had to be the punchline to a bad joke she was playing on him.

Joe looked as confused as Jimmy felt. "But why?" he asked.

"Why? They met. The old bat liked him." Maggie tousled Jimmy's hair, a half-hearted attempt to show affection. Then she wrinkled her nose, as if she had just caught a whiff of an unpleasant odor. She took a few steps away from Jimmy and lit another cigarette. "He's a likeable kid. Who knows? Who cares? Joe, this is a good thing."

But how could that be? Nora Dinsmoor *hadn't* met Jimmy, hadn't even caught a glimpse of him, as far as Joe could tell. He shook his head slowly, trying to make sense of the seemingly illogical motives that ruled Nora Driggers Dinsmoor's actions. "She's nuts," was the best he could do.

"They're all nuts up there. That's what real

money does,'' Maggie said, sounding like such an authority on the subject that Joe was almost ready to believe her. She sidled over and draped her arms around his neck. ''Dinsmoor's not dangerous, a little wacky maybe. Joe, Joey, please!'' she wheedled. ''There's no bad side here.''

But Joe was still stuck on the oddness of the request. ''How'd she even . . . ?'' His voice broke off as he replayed in his mind what had happened at Paradiso Perduto. He told Maggie, ''Dinsmoor never met Jimmy. She wouldn't open the door.''

Maggie threw herself down on the threadbare couch and angrily punched one of the pillows. ''What is it? You like our life? You like living with the dead people down here?'' she demanded of her husband.

Jimmy knew it was time to make himself scarce. Maggie was hunkering down for a fight, and he knew who was going to win. For once, he was on her side because it meant he'd be seeing Estella again. But he didn't want to watch her take Joe on, nor did he want to get caught in the middle. He grabbed his sketchpad and sneaked off before they could notice that he was leaving.

''You owe me this, Joe,'' were the last words he heard Maggie say before he closed the door to his bedroom. He settled himself on the bed and closed his eyes, recalling the details of Estella's face: her big blue eyes, rosy cheeks, pale pink skin, a mouth that made him think of strawberries. He picked up a pencil and began to draw. An hour passed, then another. Jimmy's hand flew as he tried to capture Estella on paper.

Dissatisfied with his efforts, he crumpled up one sheet after another, until the floor around the bed was littered with discarded renderings of Estella's face. When his fingers began to cramp, he stopped briefly to shake out his hands. He thought about Estella: the sound of her voice, her expression, her nasty, teasing manner. She had seemed so proud, so sure of herself, as if she had always been told she was a very special person. Yet she'd also had a sadness about her, and he'd felt that deep inside she was very, very angry. He felt the anger somehow had to do with him, which didn't make sense, since they'd never met before.

He bent back over the sketchpad and began again, now recalling the look in her eyes when she'd said, "Shower before you come next time." He drew her as a beautiful and haughty princess, surrounded by a lush jungle, addressing her invisible subjects.

Finally, he was done. He put down the pencil and studied his portrait. He thought, *Yes, that's how she looked.* Exhausted now, he closed his sketchpad and turned on the television. He suddenly became aware that he was biting his nails. The convict had said that nice hands were the sign of a gentleman. He balled his hands to keep from biting and wondered whether Estella had noticed his ragged, uneven nails.

He began flipping through the channels, stopping now and then as one program or another caught his attention. There were lots of cartoons, boring repeats of old TV series, home shopping channels, and a talk show on which two women who used to be best friends were screaming at each other because one had stolen the other's husband. He switched to the local news to get the baseball scores, but it was too early for the sports report. He pushed the mute button and watched the screen, almost as if he were watching a silent movie.

A reporter was standing in front of one of the bridges that crossed the bay, pointing to six police cars that were parked at the foot of the bridge. The camera panned to the bay, then focused in on a knot of policemen who were hauling a man out of the water. Jimmy leaned forward and held his breath, waiting to see the man's face. He had his head down and away from the television cameras as a pair of handcuffs was snapped around his wrists. The cops led him to one of the squad cars and pushed him into the back seat.

Just at the last moment, before the car door closed on him, the man looked up. He stared directly into the cameras, his face impassive, his mouth set in a grim line that told nothing, his eyes seeming to lock on Jimmy's.

I didn't tell anyone, mister, Jimmy thought. *Cross my heart and hope to die, I didn't tell one single soul.*

They arrived at Paradiso Perduto at exactly three minutes before three on Saturday afternoon. They would have been even earlier except that Maggie had made Joe drive up and back the long road that led to the house because, she said, they didn't want to seem too eager by showing up too soon. This time, Jimmy had ridden up front in the cab of the truck, stuck between Maggie and Joe, feeling very squirmy and uncomfortable in his new clothes. On Thursday, Maggie had dragged him to Sears and bought him a tan cotton suit, a madras short-sleeved shirt, and brown lace-up shoes that squeaked when he walked. He'd taken a long shower right after lunch and carefully combed his hair. But Maggie couldn't stop fussing over him, picking imaginary pieces of thread off his suit and running her fingers through his hair.

"You look sharp," she said, as the truck came to a stop in front of the mansion.

"Thanks." Jimmy tried to smile, but he was so nervous that his brain seemed to have stopped communicating with his lip muscles.

"How do I smell?" he asked, voicing his most important worry.

Maggie sniffed the top of his head. "Clean," she assured him. She unlocked the door and said, "Well, it's tea time."

He slid out behind her. Maggie had bought herself some new clothes at Sears—a red sundress and matching sandals—with some of the money Mrs. Dinsmoor had paid Joe. And she'd made Joe put on a clean white shirt, even though they were only going to walk him as far as the door. But people judged by appearances, Maggie had said to Joe, and you never knew what kind of impression you were making. This could be their big chance, she'd declared. *Chance for what?* Jimmy had wondered.

He could see now that Uncle Joe would just as soon stay in the truck, but Aunt Maggie had insisted that the two of them walk him as far as the front gate. Although Jimmy suspected she was hoping to be invited inside the mansion, for once Uncle Joe had put his foot down and told her that if Mrs. Dinsmoor had wanted them to come on in, she would have said so on the phone.

"Holy shit!" Maggie exclaimed, her eyes widening in amazement as she took in the estate. As if realizing anew the importance of Jimmy's visit, she said, "Now be polite. Yes, ma'am. No, ma'am."

He nodded his head. "I will." That must have made fifteen times today she'd reminded him to watch his manners. He wondered whether anyone ever reminded Estella to be polite.

"James, you okay?" asked Uncle Joe.

He nodded again, although he wasn't feeling so great. His stomach was hurting, and he was wishing he hadn't eaten that second hot dog for lunch.

Maggie said, "He's great." She gave him a gentle push in the direction of the mansion. "Go ahead, hon. Make us proud."

Jimmy's feet felt stuck to the ground, and for a moment, he wasn't sure they could carry him through the gate. He took a deep breath and remembered how the convict had hung on to the skiff's propeller just out of sight of the police boat, how he'd swum off into the cold and dark. All *he* had to do was play with a dumb girl, and if things got really bad, he could always leave, hitch a ride back to Cortez.

He picked up one foot, then the other, and slowly trudged toward the mansion. He stared up at it, so dazzling white in the sunlight. So big! How could two people live in such a big house?

"Ask 'em if they know how to smoke a swordfish!" Uncle Joe called out.

Jimmy grinned and felt much more cheerful. In a few hours he'd be back home, wearing his old familiar clothes, hanging around the boat with Uncle Joe. How bad could an afternoon with Princess Estella possibly be?

He walked up the steps and stood in front of the two-story, wrought-iron door. He peered between the ornate metal scrollwork, through which he could see the heavily shadowed entrance hall. He looked around for a bell, for a place to knock on the door. Finding neither, he moved closer to the door and said, ''Hello?''

His voice echoed weakly in the cavernous entryway.

He cleared his voice and tried again, more loudly. ''Is anybody—?''

Suddenly, Estella appeared on the other side of the door. ''Who is it?'' she demanded, although he knew she could see him as clearly as he could see her.

''Jimmy,'' he said and fought the impulse to stick his tongue out at her.

''What's the secret password?''

He searched his memory but could remember hearing nothing of the sort. Did this mean he would be turned away from Paradiso Perduto, banished from the realm of the beautiful Princess Estella? ''No one told me about a secret password,'' he said.

Estella pushed the door open. She was wearing a bright pink suit that looked more like something a grown-up would wear than a child. Jimmy had never seen a girl his age dressed in anything similar. She looked rather silly, yet at the same time quite beautiful.

"Why, it's Jimmy the Geek." She giggled and held her nose.

He knew he didn't smell. She was just being nasty again. "Esmella de Vil," he shot back at her and boldly marched into the mansion.

The entrance hall felt and looked more like an underground jungle cave than a room in a house. Tree branches had poked through gaping holes in the large, shattered picture window. Shards of glass littered the floor, and leafy vines twisted and spilled across the walls.

Estella seemed oblivious to the chaos. She sauntered across the two-by-four planks that had been laid over the vegetation-covered floor, and proceeded to give Jimmy a tour of the mansion. "The design of this tile floor was taken from the Alhambra in Spain," she recited, as if she were reading from a guide book.

Jimmy followed her, balancing on the wooden planks. He knew that Spain was a country in Europe, but he'd never heard of the Alhambra, and he couldn't see anything that even resembled a tile beneath all the dense green moss that lay underfoot.

She pointed upward. Still affecting her museum-tour-guide tone, she said, "The ceiling is gold leaf. Real gold. It's exactly like the 'thousand-wing' ceiling from the Accademia in Venice, Italy."

He raised his eyes, searching for gold, but could find not a trace of it through the darkness. He was tempted to ask her about the Accademia and its thousand-wing ceiling, because it sounded so interesting. Instead, he nodded and kept quiet, because he was afraid of her sharp tongue. He wondered how she knew so much. Was it because her aunt was so rich? Did she have shelves and shelves of wonderful books that were illustrated with pictures of all the places she was describing? Or perhaps she'd actually travelled to Spain and Italy and seen those places for herself. He didn't think he'd ever met anyone before who'd been to Europe.

As Estella led him deeper into the ruined mansion, he caught glimpses of barely visible creatures slipping around the corners. He glanced at his feet, imagining mice or lizards skittering against his ankles. Estella gave no sign that she saw or heard anything. She was apparently accustomed to sharing her home with these four-legged invaders.

Now she was climbing up a circular double staircase. Elaborately carved angels and devils waged gory battle with one another all along the marble bannister. Jimmy reached over and touched the horns on one of the devils; his finger came away blackened with the dirt of ages. As much to break the silence as out of curiosity, he said, "What does Paradiso Perduto mean?"

"Paradise Lost," she said, sounding annoyed that he should have to ask so obvious a question. "You don't speak Italian?"

He shook his head. "No."

"I speak three languages. Not including English, of course."

"I speak Spanish," he said. Then, worried that Spanish might be one of her three languages and she would catch him in his half-lie, he hedged, "A little."

She turned as she reached the top of the stairway and stared at him in alarm. "You're not Cuban, are you?"

"No," he began. "But—"

"Good." She cut him off before he had a chance to mention that his best friend was Cuban, which was how he knew a few words of Spanish.

He quickly decided not to tell her about Gilberto. Grateful that she seemed, temporarily at least, to have run out of rude questions, he followed her through a maze of long, damp, unlit corridors. Although the halls were so gloomy that he often had to reach his hand out and touch the wall to keep from stumbling, she walked swiftly and confidently, almost as if she could see in the dark. Why was there no electricity, he wondered. Why were there no lamps to light the way?

She stopped abruptly in front of a closed door that smelled of rotting wood and said, "Well, go ahead."

He could hear music playing inside the room, a loud, brassy Latin rhythm. He felt reluctant to open the door. Even his recent encounter with the convict had not seemed as strange and terrifying as the possibility that Paradiso Perduto might be haunted by any number of ghosts and hobgoblins. "Aren't you coming?" he asked, figuring there was safety in numbers.

"Quel sot," she declared.

He didn't need to know which of her several languages she was using to understand that she had insulted him. He didn't bother asking for a translation as she spun around on her heels and skipped down the hallway.

Jimmy took a deep breath and thought about how he'd lied to the police to save the convict. He'd seen from the convict's eyes that the man had appreciated his courage. He drew on that courage now as he knocked on the door.

There was no answer.

He knocked again, more loudly this time. The door swung open.

A young woman, whom he guessed to be no more than eighteen or nineteen, stood with her back to him. She was dressed in an outfit from an earlier decade: white stretch pants and a colorful flowered shirt. She ignored him as she danced to the disco rhythms of the music, swaying back and forth in time to the beat.

"Ah, excuse me," he said. "I—"

The young woman twirled around. Jimmy barely stifled a gasp of shock at the sight that confronted him: the face of a woman who had to be at least sixty years old, an aged woman with the body of a teenager. Her hair was bleached blond and sprayed into a tight little flip, and he could barely make out her features beneath her heavy mask of makeup. Heavy diamond earrings, shaped like chandeliers, tugged at her earlobes; they bobbed hypnotically as she flitted about the room, wailing a duet with the singer whose record she was playing.

She looked like she was dressed up for Halloween, but this was only the middle of May. Jimmy took a few steps back as she danced toward him. He didn't care how rich Nora Driggers Dinsmoor was. All he had to do was look at her to know she was crazy.

CHAPTER 4

Shrilly serenading him, Mrs. Dinsmoor advanced toward him, almost as if she were pursuing him. Without giving any thought to what he was doing, Jimmy kept stepping backward, trying to put distance between them, until he felt something solid bump up against his legs, and he realized she'd cornered him against her bed.

The record ended. The room was quiet for a moment, except for the sound of Mrs. Dinsmoor panting to catch her breath. Close up, he saw that beneath all her spooky-looking makeup she was quite attractive, for an older lady. But she was definitely weird, and so were her niece and her mansion.

She stared at him with huge round eyes ringed with white circles. "Who're you?" she asked as she reached out a hand to steady herself.

"Jimmy, ma'am," he said.

"Why are you in my bedroom, Jimmy?" she asked, sounding genuinely puzzled.

It was a good question, and he wished he had an answer that made sense. The fact was he didn't have the faintest idea why he was here. All he knew was that he wanted to leave as quickly as possible, but he wasn't sure he could find his way to the front door without Estella to guide him.

Another record dropped onto the turntable. A different singer was warbling his version of "Besame Mucho," the same song that had been playing before.

"Here," said Mrs. Dinsmoor. She draped her bony arm around his shoulder. "Help me to bed."

She weighed almost nothing. She felt lighter than some fish he had caught. He half-carried her past the footboard—a giant carved angel with widespread, gilded wings—and helped her settle onto the bed.

She lowered herself against the pillows with a sigh, then said, "Give me your hand."

Her skin was dry and paper-thin, like a butterfly's wings. Her fingers felt like a skeleton's bones. She clamped his hand across her left breast and held it there forcibly when he tried to pull away.

"What is this?" she asked wearily.

"Your . . . your boob?" he stammered. He knew he must be blushing bright red. The closest he'd ever come before to touching a woman's breast was the time he'd sneaked up on Gloria Rhinebold and brushed his hand across her chest before she'd swatted him away.

"My heart," she whispered. "My heart. It's broken. Can you feel that?"

He couldn't feel much besides a flat little pancake-shaped mound. "I'm sorry," he said, although he wasn't sure what he was apologizing for.

She let go of his hand. He shifted awkwardly from one leg to the other. What next, he wondered. He'd been invited over to play with Estella, but she'd vanished, leaving him alone to deal with Mrs. Dancing Dinsmoor.

He was about to ask where Estella was when an enormous mass of fur suddenly flew at his face.

He yelled, "Argh!" and smacked it away.

The fur ball landed on Mrs. Dinsmoor's bed, leaped into her arms, and let out a shrill meow.

"Wow! That's the biggest cat I've ever seen." He leaned over and cautiously patted the animal's back. The cat arched its back and hissed. Jimmy heeded the warning and quickly backed away. "What do you feed it?"

"Other cats," Mrs. Dinsmoor sounded so serious that he almost believed her. "You might as well proceed," she said. "Go ahead, dance," she ordered him with an imperious wave of her hand.

"What?" He thought maybe he'd misheard her.

"I'd like you to dance," she calmly reiterated.

He stared at her, too astonished to say a word.

Mrs. Dinsmoor cradled the monster cat against her chest and smiled grimly. "Why do you think you're here?" she demanded.

He was about to admit he didn't know himself why he'd been summoned to her home. But she cut him off before he could open his mouth to speak. "To entertain me," she answered her own question. "So, please, go ahead. Dance. Anything. Pony, fox trot, frug, Philly dog, fandango . . ."

For reasons he couldn't understand, he felt ashamed of himself, as if he'd done something wrong. As if he'd deliberately misled her, somehow tricked her into inviting him into her bedroom. Unable to meet her gaze, he hung his head and said softly, "I'm sorry. I can't."

She shook her head so violently that her diamond earrings clattered like wind chimes. "Can't?" she snorted. "Or won't?" She snapped her fingers furiously. "Dance!" she commanded him again. Her body was twitching so violently that he half-expected her arms and legs and head to separate themselves from her torso and go flying about the room. "Dance!" she shrieked. "Dance!"

There was no use explaining that he didn't know how. He felt he had no choice but to try and please her. Her mad-eyed gaze made him feel all the more awkward and self-conscious, so he dropped his head and began shuffling his feet in a clumsy attempt to imitate his aunt and uncle's dancing. But it was hopeless. His feet felt like leaden weights. His hands, too, felt heavy and incapable of moving in any sort of graceful way. After only a few seconds, he gave up and stopped moving.

"Get out of here!" Mrs. Dinsmoor said furiously.

Near tears, he begged her, "Please don't tell my aunt."

"I'm bored, and you're useless." She spat out the words as if she were accusing him of a hideous crime. "Useless! I'll tell her exactly what you are," she threatened. "She can forget any remuneration. In fact, I might just sue her for—"

"Wait!" Jimmy cried. He desperately cast about for a way to appease Mrs. Dinsmoor, to keep her from making good on her threat. If he failed in his task here at Paradiso Perduto,

Maggie would never forgive him. There had to be *something* he could do to amuse her. "I can—"

"Dance?" she asked hopefully.

He shook his head. Then inspiration hit him. "Draw," he said. "I can draw."

She studied him for a moment, as if deciding whether or not to accept his offer. She yawned. Then she said, sounding bored, "Fine. Draw me."

There was just one problem, however. "I don't have my pad."

He had expected her to summon Estella to bring him paper and pencils. But Mrs. Dinsmoor was not the kind of person to do the expected. She glanced around the room until her gaze fell on a book that was lying on the floor next to her bed. "*Salome*," it said on the cover of the book, which looked to be very old and very valuable. "By Oscar Wilde."

She picked up the book, carelessly ripped out the title page, and handed it to him. "Here. And you can use my lipstick and eyeliner. Over there on the dressing table. *Allez, allez!*"

He had no idea what her last two words meant, but her tone sounded urgent enough that he did as he was told without asking any questions. He walked over to the dressing table, dragging his feet like a doomed man marching to his execution. The top of the table was heaped with piles of dirty tissues, hair

clips and bobby pins, clumps of Mrs. Dinsmoor's bleached blond hair, more kinds of
makeup than he'd ever seen even in Maggie's
considerable collection. He rooted about
among the tubes and containers until he'd
found suitable tools, which included several
different colors of lipstick and pencils for the
lips and eyebrows.

He tested one of the lipsticks on his fingertip. It felt greasy and thick, and it wasn't at all
what he was used to, but he supposed that it
would do, in an emergency. And this, he decided, was definitely an emergency.

Mrs. Dinsmoor was now reclining against
her pillows, her arms spread above her head.
Jimmy sat down on the floor, crossed his legs,
and studied her in preparation for drawing her
portrait.

She seemed to enjoy his scrutiny. "What do
you think of me?" she demanded. "Of my
house?"

He weighed her question carefully, trying to
formulate in his mind an accurate description.
"It's . . ."

"Does it scare you?" she interrupted.

"No," he said truthfully. He'd stopped feeling scared as soon as she'd begun talking to
him, when he'd realized that she was just another lonely person, a person odder than most
who happened to have a lot more money than

anyone else he knew. "It makes me . . . sad," he admitted.

She nodded, as if he'd given her the correct answer. "Yes," she said, sounding almost pleased. "It's a sad place."

She closed her eyes and fell silent. She lay so absolutely still that he would have thought she'd fallen asleep except that with one hand, she very slowly stroked her cat, who lay equally still and silent. Jimmy began to draw, using a brown eyebrow pencil to sketch the outlines of her eyes. As always, he soon became so absorbed in what he was doing that he lost all sense of time.

The record ended. Another began to play. Then it, too, ended. The room grew quiet, but Jimmy heard neither the music nor the silence that followed. Shadows deepened in the dusty room as the afternoon stretched toward evening, but he hardly noticed. Finally, he was finished. He smoothed out the page and assessed his work. It might not be his best effort, but it was certainly far from his worst. He looked up at Mrs. Dinsmoor, then back at his drawing. Then he stood up and held it out to her.

"Here," he said.

He'd drawn her eyes. They stared out at her from the otherwise blank page, her beautiful brown eyes, so troubled and tormented.

She gave no indication whether she was pleased with what he'd done, but he was satisfied. If Mrs. Dinsmoor's eyes were the windows to her soul, then what he'd discovered in their depths was sad beyond words. And now that sadness had been captured on paper.

She didn't react, gave no indication of how she felt. All she said was, "Go outside and call for Estella."

She continued to stare at the page as he walked across the room to the doorway.

"Estella?" he called, his voice echoing off the walls. "Estella?"

As usual, she seemed to appear out of nowhere. Suddenly, there she was, standing in the previously empty hall. She glanced at him angrily for no apparent reason. As she slipped past him, all she said was, "Excuse me."

Paralyzed by her icy cold beauty, he stared after her.

"Is tea ready?" she asked her aunt.

"I want you to sit for a portrait," Mrs. Dinsmoor said.

Estella pirouetted across the room to gaze at herself in the mirror that hung above the dresser. She floated her arms up above her head and struck a pose. "A portrait?" she asked, seemingly pleased with what she saw reflected back at her. "By whom?"

Mrs. Dinsmoor pointed to Jimmy. "This boy."

"The gardener dork?" Estella laughed scornfully. She swept her arms down and extended them out by her sides as she performed a graceful plié. Her performance completed, she said, "I'll be in my room."

Mrs. Dinsmoor raised her voice slightly. "Pull over the chair from my dressing table and sit there."

Estella ignored her request. "I'll be in my room," she said.

As she began walking toward the door, Jimmy waited for Mrs. Dinsmoor to reprimand Estella for her rudeness. But rather than scold the girl, Mrs. Dinsmoor said softly, "Please."

Estella stopped and turned to look at Mrs. Dinsmoor. No words were spoken by either one, but they seemed to be communicating in a silent language known only to the two of them. After several seconds, during which Jimmy held his breath, Estella grudgingly sat down on the chair. She folded her hands on her lap, stuck her chin in the air, and stared defiantly at Jimmy, as if to say, *Draw me if you dare.*

"You sit by me," Mrs. Dinsmoor told Jimmy, motioning him to join her on the bed.

Now it was his turn to obey with reluctance. He climbed up onto the bed, taking care to put as much space as possible between himself and the old woman. Up close, she looked even more frightening and freakish: all skin and bones beneath the thick layers of makeup, the bright red lips, the sorrowful eyes ringed with black. As she ripped another blank page out of *Salome* and handed it to him, the cat fixed Jimmy with a baleful eye and bared its teeth in a lion-sized yawn.

Jimmy pushed away his fears of being mauled to death by the cat and concentrated on drawing Estella. She sat unmoving, as regal and stationary as if she were cast in marble. He was both fascinated and terrified by her, but his hand was steady as he captured the shape of her lips, the curve of her neck, the cold, imperious expression on her face. Of all her features, her eyes were the most difficult to re-create on paper. He could find no feeling in their depths, no sense of who she was or what she was thinking.

Estella wasn't like any other child he knew, and not simply because she lived in a ruined old mansion with a very rich old aunt. She behaved, spoke, and dressed more like an adult than a child, so that it was hard to imagine her running around, playing games like tag or hide-and-seek, going fishing or hanging out at the beach. He wondered whether she had any friends and how she spent her days.

Mrs. Dinsmoor peered at the drawing over his shoulder. "She is beautiful, isn't she?" she whispered.

"Don't talk about me in front of the boy," Estella snapped, without moving a muscle in her face.

Mrs. Dinsmoor ignored her niece. "What do you think of her? Come on, whisper it in my ear," she coaxed Jimmy.

He put down the eyeliner pencil he'd been using and flexed his fingers. The old lady really seemed to want his opinion, and after all the mean things Estella had said to him, he was happy to give it. He leaned closer to Mrs. Dinsmoor and almost choked on the smell of dead flowers that she wore like perfume.

"Well?" she prompted him.

"I think she's a snob," he whispered, noticing that she had taped her cheeks to the flesh behind her ears so that the skin on her face looked tighter than it actually was.

"Anything else?"

"I think she's really pretty," he admitted.

"Anything else?"

"I don't think she likes me," he said sadly.

Mrs. Dinsmoor smiled happily. "But you love her," she declared.

Jimmy couldn't disagree with her. She was right. He *did* love Estella, though in a very different way from how he loved Uncle Joe, or even Aunt Maggie. He wanted to make her laugh. He wanted to bring her to his private island and show her the pieces of driftwood that washed up on the beach after a storm, and the barracudas leaping through the water. He wanted to protect her from whatever was making her so angry and unhappy. He wanted to take care of her.

As if reading his mind, Mrs. Dinsmoor said, "She'll only break your heart. It's a fact. Tragic. You're already in love with her, and even though I warn you, I guarantee you that this girl will hurt you terribly, you'll still pursue her. Ain't love grand?" She clapped her hands and laughed gleefully.

"I'd like to go now," Jimmy said, frightened by her malevolence.

"Are you finished?" Mrs. Dinsmoor demanded.

"Before I'm a teenager, please," Estella said snidely.

He added a few more lines to her hair and decided that yes, he was finished. Handing the paper to Mrs. Dinsmoor, he repeated, "I'd like to go now."

Mrs. Dinsmoor glanced at his work but made no comment. "Estella," she said, "see Jimmy out." As he scrambled off the bed, she put a restraining hand on his arm. "Would you like to come again?"

Yes. No. Maybe. Soon. Never. His feelings were knocking around in his brain like a rack of bowling pins.

"Would you like to see Estella again?" she said softly.

He felt like a hooked fish wiggling on the

line. "Yes," he said finally, because he couldn't bear to say no.

Mrs. Dinsmoor chuckled. "Poor boy," she said, and handed him an envelope. "Give this to your guardian." She passed the drawing over to Estella. "And this is yours, dear."

Without so much as glancing at the paper, Estella crumpled it up into a ball and threw it at the sleeping cat. Then she turned and smiled at Jimmy, as if to say, *That's what I think about your drawing.*

He didn't care, he told himself. It wasn't a very good drawing, and who cared about her opinion anyway? He looked at the envelope, thought about how heavy it felt in his hand. The flap was sealed shut, but he guessed that Mrs. Dinsmoor had stuck a wad of cash inside. He itched to send the envelope flying in the same direction as the drawing. But he restrained himself, because he knew what Maggie would do to him if she ever found out that he'd behaved rudely to Mrs. Dinsmoor, let alone tossed away a pile of money.

He shoved the envelope into his pocket and followed Estella, retracing his steps down the grand, curving staircase. At the bottom of the steps was a marble water fountain, which Jimmy hadn't noticed earlier. Estella stopped there now and said, "One sec."

She leaned over, took a long drink, then straightened up. "Want some?"

In fact, he *was* thirsty. But he stubbornly didn't want to say yes to her, even if all she was offering was something as simple as a few sips of water.

He shook his head. "No, thanks."

"It's not poisoned," she said, her lip curling with ill-disguised disdain.

"I know that," he said. He glared at her, thinking, *You're not so tough.* But she sure was pretty. Part of him wanted to go running out of the mansion as quickly as his feet could carry him. Another part wanted to grab Estella by the hand and spend the rest of the afternoon exploring the estate together with her.

She was glaring back at him. Once again, he could read nothing in her eyes. "You're scared," she declared.

"I am not," he shot back. To prove it, he walked over to the fountain and swallowed a mouthful of water. Suddenly, Estella's mouth was next to his, her lips parted to catch the arcing stream. Her tongue flickered across the spray of water and touched his tongue, and then their lips were touching, and she was kissing him. Then, just as suddenly, she stepped back and made a big show of licking away the few drops of water that clung to her lips.

Without realizing it, Jimmy put his hand to his mouth and touched the spot where their lips had met. He'd never kissed a girl before. Or had she kissed him? And why would she have done such a thing?

She was skipping ahead of him now, looking over her shoulder, laughing at his obvious confusion. He wanted to call out to her, *Wait! Tell me why you did that!* But he knew better. She would only throw her head back and laugh and say something cruel that would make him feel stupider than he already did.

As he trailed her to the main road, he tried to come up with a clever parting comment. But he wasn't as practiced as Estella in finding just the right words to wound or insult. Frustrated, he kicked at the pebbles that lay beneath his feet and wished he had never laid eyes on Estella or her crazy old aunt.

They reached the gate. Joe's truck was waiting on the other side. Jimmy turned to Estella, opened his mouth to say good-bye. But typically, she had the last word.

"Don't call us," she said. "We'll call you."

Maggie had to know every detail of how he'd spent his afternoon. What did Mrs. Dinsmoor look like? Was she old or young? Fat or thin? What was she wearing? What did she offer him for tea? Was there a butler or a maid to serve and clear away the dishes? And the mansion . . . how was it decorated? Did it resemble any of the homes she'd seen on "Lifestyles of the Rich and Famous"?

Certain she would never believe the truth,

since he could hardly believe it himself and he'd been there, Jimmy answered as briefly as possible. But in his attempt to avoid the facts without telling outright lies, he succeeded in annoying Maggie so much that she stopped speaking to him and picked a fight with Joe before they were even halfway home. All that prevented her from going into a full-blown rant were the five hundred dollars that Mrs. Dinsmoor had handed Jimmy in the envelope.

Five hundred dollars! He'd done nothing to earn it except draw Estella's portrait and put up with her insults. Except that the money immediately disappeared into Maggie's pocket, Jimmy would have felt almost rich.

But not rich enough. As he sat alone at the table, eating chili out of a can for supper, he looked around the kitchen and tried to see it through Estella's critical eyes: the rusted refrigerator, the broken light fixture that Joe kept promising to fix, the cupboard that was missing a door, the chipped linoleum.

"Where's our floor from?" he asked Maggie and Joe, who were eating their chili in front of the TV.

Maggie rolled her eyes at him, and even Joe stared at him as if he might have a loose screw before they both went back to watching "Wheel of Fortune."

Yeah, he supposed it was kind of a dumb question. He swallowed another spoonful of chili and pondered an even dumber one: What was Estella having for supper tonight?

Six days passed without another invitation to Paradiso Perduto. Maggie hardly left the apartment for fear she would miss Mrs. Dinsmoor's phone call. She repeatedly grilled Jimmy about what had transpired at the mansion: Hadn't Mrs. Dinsmoor all but promised she would invite him back? Could she have changed her mind because he'd done something to offend Estella? Had he behaved himself with Estella, played nicely, minded his table manners, said please and thank you very much, I had a good time?

Bottom line, demanded Maggie, why hadn't they heard from the old lady?

When Joe jokingly pointed out that she was acting like a lovesick teenager waiting to be asked out on a second date, Maggie blew up at both of them, told Joe he could sleep on the couch, and retreated into their bedroom. He was a loser, she yelled from behind the locked door. Always had been, always would be. And he was raising Jimmy to be a loser, too. Neither one of them was smart enough to recognize a good thing when they saw it. Mrs. Dinsmoor was an opportunity waiting to happen, a chance for them to make enough money that they could move out of their miserable hellhole of an apartment and find a decent place to live.

Joe put a finger to his lips, warning Jimmy to keep quiet, though he didn't need much reminding. When Maggie was in one of her moods, it was best to let the storm run its course.

She was screeching so loudly that she missed hearing the phone ring. Joe had to pound on the door to ask her, could she put a lid on it, please, so he could speak to Mrs. Dinsmoor. And when he informed her, a minute later, that Jimmy had been invited back, she emerged from her room, all smiles. They were going out for dinner, she announced. They could order whatever they wanted—steak, lobster, the sky was the limit. Because Mrs. Dinsmoor was picking up the tab.

The dancing lessons were Mrs. Dinsmoor's idea, of course. The mere mention of the idea threw Jimmy into a heart-stopping panic, while Estella made a big show of yawning and looked bored. Undeterred, Mrs. Dinsmoor marched them off to the ballroom, which was in the same state of decay and disorder as the rest of the mansion. She instructed them to face each other in the middle of the room and made herself comfortable on a gold-leafed chaise, one of the few pieces of furniture that had withstood the attack of the elements.

She clapped her hands, a signal that class was in session. "Now, what do you say?" she prompted Jimmy, who was trembling with nervousness from standing in such close proximity to Estella.

He chewed on his thumbnail and pondered her question. "Hello?" he finally replied.

"Dope," Estella muttered under her breath.

Mrs. Dinsmoor sighed audibly as she dragged herself off the chaise and skipped over to where Jimmy was standing. " 'May I have the pleasure of this dance?' That's what you say," she instructed him. " 'May I have the pleasure of this dance?' Now you."

Jimmy nodded. He was fed up with Estella's name-calling, and he was going to prove to her that he could learn to dance just as well as any of her fancy Sarasota boyfriends. "May I have the pleasure of this dance?" he said, mimicking Mrs. Dinsmoor's inflection.

"Do you know how?" Estella said disdainfully.

Determined not to show his hurt feelings, he bit his lip and allowed Mrs. Dinsmoor to place his arm around Estella's waist. He could feel Estella stiffen beneath his touch. She glared at a spot in the distance and refused to meet his gaze as Mrs. Dinsmoor began clapping her hands in a slow-moving rhythm. He shuffled his feet left and right, forward and back, simultaneously trying to imitate Estella's moves and avoid stepping on her feet. When he landed squarely on her toes, she grimaced conspicuously and moved away from him.

But Mrs. Dinsmoor shook her head no. Her mind was made up. She gently steered the girl back into place and recommended her clapping. No matter what Estella thought or felt about it, Jimmy would learn how to dance.

CHAPTER 5

Jimmy's visits to Paradiso Perduto—and the dance lessons—continued once a week for the next seven years. His encounter with the convict had become a distant memory, an event that he only rarely thought about. Estella, on the other hand, preoccupied a very large part of his consciousness. At ten, he'd had an innocent puppy-love crush on her; at seventeen, he was so madly in love that at times he couldn't breathe for wanting her.

His world was neatly divided into two distinct and disparate parts. Six days a week were spent in Cortez—going to school, fishing, helping Uncle Joe on his boat, hanging out with his friends. But on the seventh day, which he almost invariably spent in Sarasota, he belonged to Mrs. Dinsmoor and Estella.

Their relationship had changed and evolved

over the years, but some aspects of it remained constant. Mrs. Dinsmoor still handed him an envelope full of money at the end of each visit. And Estella still behaved as if it were her God-given right to humiliate and abuse him.

By now, her insults felt so commonplace to Jimmy that he hardly heard them. Her harsh words had become part of the background noise at Paradiso Perduto, as familiar as the dilapidated condition of the mansion, the riot-ous, weed-choked state of the grounds sur-rounding it. He no longer felt pain when she mocked him; he almost welcomed the hurtful comments because it meant she noticed him. She cared enough about him to be nasty.

Estella at seventeen was a full-blown beauty. When he occasionally went into town with her to run an errand for Mrs. Dinsmoor, he no-ticed—even if she didn't—how other men turned to stare at her as she passed. They stared at him, too, and their expressions were easy to read: *You lucky bastard,* he could see them thinking. *How did you land such a fox?*

In fact, he was more likely to get elected President of the United States than to wind up with Estella. But a guy could dream. And if nothing else, he still got to dance with her.

After all those afternoons of practicing under Mrs. Dinsmoor's demanding supervision, Jimmy had become an accomplished dancer. Even Mrs. Dinsmoor seemed to think so.

"And you said you couldn't dance." She laughed, applauding him and Estella from her usual perch on the gold-leafed chaise as they twirled their way across the parquet floor to a dramatic finish.

They made a great team—for as long as the music was playing and they were swinging and swaying and anticipating each other's moves. The record over, they faced each other, their cheeks flushed, their eyes shining. She'd seemed in an especially good mood, which he'd dared to hope had something to do with him. He bowed to her and came up with flourish. She smiled as she sank down into a deep, graceful curtsey. And then Estella pushed her hair away from her face and began walking toward the door.

Jimmy looked at his watch. It was still early, just past three-thirty.

Mrs. Dinsmoor apparently had the same thought. "Where are you going, dear?" she asked. Her voice echoed through the cavernous ballroom as she adjusted the lacy top she wore over her harlequin-patterned capezio stretch pants.

"I have to get ready," Estella said. "There's that cocktail thing over at the Rewalds'."

Jimmy pulled a handkerchief out of his pocket and wiped his forehead. He stared at her, wondering what people did at cocktail things and how he could ever compete for Estella with the boys who spent their lives attending cocktail things at the Rewalds', whoever they might be.

Mrs. Dinsmoor obviously knew them, because she shook her head and looked disapproving. "Lane Rewald? That old gin blossom. One more cocktail and—"

"Karl Rewald," Estella said impatiently. "Lane is his father. Karl doesn't drink."

"Nonsense!" Mrs. Dinsmoor scoffed. "The whole family's pickled. Who's your escort?"

Estella hooted. "Escort? Please, it's the eighties! I'm going myself. I don't need—"

"I'll bring you," Jimmy blurted out.

Estella and Mrs. Dinsmoor stared at him. He wasn't sure who was more surprised by his offer—the two women or he himself. He'd never mentioned his dreams of going out with Estella to anyone, not even to Joe. But graduation was coming up soon, and the talk at school was all about the senior prom, who was bringing whom, who didn't yet have a date. There was no one he could imagine taking except Estella. And yet in a million years he couldn't imagine taking Estella to a high-school prom.

But a cocktail party?

"Certainly," said Mrs. Dinsmoor. "Jimmy will make a fine date."

"Oh God," Estella groaned.

But she was overruled. "Then it's done," Mrs. Dinsmoor said, snapping her fingers.

Estella made a face, stuck her tongue out at Jimmy behind her aunt's back. "Okay," she grudgingly conceded. "But you meet me there. Eleven fifteen North Ocean."

"Right," said Jimmy, too astounded by what had just happened to care about Estella's lack of enthusiasm. "Okay."

But her parting shot left him with plenty to worry about. "Wear your dinner jacket," she said.

Jimmy pushed the speed limit all the way to Cortez and broke his personal record getting home. He didn't have a moment to waste cleaning himself up, finding something to wear to the party, getting back to Sarasota on time to meet Estella. He bolted up the stairs to the apartment, dashed into his bedroom, and started tearing through his closet to find a clean white shirt and a pair of jeans.

Joe arrived home just as Jimmy was dousing himself with aftershave lotion. One look at his nephew's deer-in-the-headlights expression and Jimmy's monosyllabic explanation were all Joe needed to spring into action.

He glanced around Jimmy's room. Clothes were tossed across every surface, including the lamp next to his bed. Food-encrusted plates and empty soda cans were stacked on the dresser. Magazines, books, and tapes lay in piles all over the floor. The sole decorative touch was a portrait of Estella that Jimmy had hung on the wall facing his bed.

"How much time we got?" Joe asked as he ran for the ironing board.

"None," Jimmy moaned, giving his black shoes a quick swipe with a clean cloth. "I'm late. I'm dead."

Joe dug out his one dress shirt and the silver cuff links Maggie had given him for their tenth anniversary. While Jimmy put a crease in his jeans, Joe turned on the shower to steam out a white linen blazer that had somehow found its way into his and Maggie's closet.

When enough of the wrinkles were gone that the blazer looked presentable he brought it into the bedroom. "This'll pass for a dinner jacket."

"Where'd you get that?" asked Jimmy.

"Maggie must have forgotten it."

Jimmy tried on the blazer. The sleeves were a tad short, and there was another problem. "It's a girl's," he groaned.

"Keep it buttoned," Joe advised. "No one'll notice."

He picked up the bow tie that Jimmy had dug out of his drawer and slid it under Jimmy's collar. "You all right for money?"

Jimmy nodded. "I'm fine."

Joe fumbled with the tie. "I haven't done one of these since my wedding," he said, shaking his head. He undid it, thought for a moment, then moved behind Jimmy and started over. "Your aunt bought me a clip-on. Just not the same."

He evened out the two sides of the bow and stepped back to study his handiwork. "There. That'll have to do."

Jimmy raised his neck and touched the tie with both hands. "Thanks," he said.

"You look sharp," said Joe.

Jimmy grinned sheepishly. He couldn't remember feeling this nervous since the first time he'd stepped over the threshold at Paradiso Perduto when he was ten years old.

He crossed the room to inspect himself in the mirror. Even he had to admit it: he *did* look sharp. His hair, bleached golden blond from all the hours he spent on the boat, was slicked down and neatly combed. His skin was zit-free. He squinted at his reflection, hardly recognizing the young man staring back at him. He'd worn a tie and jacket maybe three, four times in his life. It felt odd, too confining, but he liked the visual effect. As Joe handed him the car keys, he offered up a silent prayer that Estella would, too.

The sun was just disappearing below the horizon when Jimmy drove up to the stone walls that guarded the Rewalds' mansion. A long line of Rolls-Royces, Bentleys, BMWs, and other equally ostentatious cars snaked ahead of him down the palm tree–lined driveway. Jimmy was on the verge of making a right turn through the gate when he lost his nerve. He was driving Joe's dented old wreck of a truck. How could he show up behind those high-priced wheels and not feel like a fool in front of Estella?

He switched off his turn signal and continued down the road, then came to a stop on the shoulder a block past the estate. He turned off the engine and leaned back in his seat. He thought about money and how it felt never to have quite enough when other people had so damned much that they didn't know what to do with it. He thought about Mrs. Dinsmoor, who was so rich, yet seemed so sad even on the rare occasions when he got her to laugh. He didn't know any of Estella's fancy friends, but he'd met plenty of rich folks hanging out at the dock, and they didn't appear to be much different from the people he'd grown up with in Cortez, except that they had fancier clothes and talked as if they had stones in their cheeks.

He had nothing to be ashamed of, he told himself, even if the truck was a disaster and his clothes didn't quite cut it. He was a smart enough guy, and plenty of girls at school had hinted that they'd say yes if he called them up for a date. And he sure as hell knew how to dance, he thought, laughing softly. Mrs. Dinsmoor had seen to that.

Besides, if he stood Estella up, he would never hear the end of it. He would have given her sufficient ammunition to use against him for the rest of his life. That thought alone was motive enough to get him to restart the car, make a U-turn, and drive back to the Rewalds.

The valet parking men were obviously off-duty cops. They ogled the truck suspiciously when he braked in front of the mansion, and he half-expected to be charged with breaking and entering where he wasn't invited, and hauled in for questioning. Jimmy smiled with more assurance than he was feeling as he handed over his keys.

Tugging at the too-short jacket sleeves, he walked up the path to the house. He had almost reached the stairs when his attention was caught by the unmistakable sound of someone puking his guts out. A second later, the source of the noise appeared: a pasty-faced preppie crawled out from the carefully sculpted hedge next to the path, pulled himself semi-erect, and lurched toward Jimmy. Jimmy steered clear of him and walked slowly up the steps. A glamorous young couple brushed past him into the house.

Through the open door, he could hear piano music, laughter, people talking and enjoying themselves. His feet suddenly felt nailed to the ground. He couldn't take another step forward. As much as he wanted to find Estella, he couldn't bring himself to enter the house. He didn't belong there. He knew that, and the people on the other side of the door would know it, too, as soon as they laid eyes on him.

He turned and walked back down the path, dodging the preppie who had renewed his attack on the bushes. He reclaimed his keys from the valet and got into the truck. He leaned his head on the steering wheel and wondered how he was ever going to explain his behavior to Estella.

The next thing he heard was her voice floating through the window. "You're quite an escort," she said.

He looked up and saw her coming toward him from the house.

"Yeah, well, the party looks boring," he said, ashamed of himself now that she'd caught him in the act of retreat.

She leaned into the window, her face close to his. "How would you know?" she demanded.

He grinned weakly and gave her the only excuse he could come up with on such short notice. "Someone barfs on the doorstep on the way *in*—it's a bad sign. One of my rules."

"You have a better idea?"

He stared at her and wondered for the millionth time how she really felt about him. She stared back at him unblinkingly.

"We could . . . take a ride," he said hesitantly.

Her lips twitched as if she were trying to suppress a smile. Was it purely his imagination, or did her eyes soften, as if she had read his mind and understood—perhaps better than he did—what he was really saying? Her response was simple and pointed. "Where?"

His mouth went dry. He could feel his pulse beating at the base of his throat. She seemed to understand that he was beyond speech, and finally, she answered for him.

"How about your place?"

The drive home, with Estella sitting next to him, felt like the longest ride he'd ever taken. He could hardly tear his eyes away from her long enough to focus on the road. She'd lit up a cigarette as soon as she'd slid into the truck, and he'd almost said, like a jerk, "I didn't know you smoked."

As if he had a right to care about anything she did. . . .

But he did care, very much. He wanted to know everything about her. He wanted this night to go on forever, to marry her and be with her always. He wanted to take her away to his island and spend the rest of their lives there together. He was sure he could make her happy, if only she would let him.

She was so beautiful, even more so tonight

than usual, if that were possible. She'd tied her hair back with a clip, leaving only a few wispy tendrils to fall about her face. She was wearing a simple black dress with thin straps that showed off her bare shoulders and arms. The dress was cut low enough in front that he couldn't look at her without getting a hard-on. She'd kicked off her high heels and curled her legs up under her, so that he could see flashes of her thigh whenever she moved. Her lips puckered around the cigarette; she inhaled deeply and played nervously with the single strand of pearls around her neck.

"They're all stupid drunks," she said, staring straight ahead through the windshield, as if she were watching the traffic. "Their idea of cool is to drive Daddy's Lotus into the Intracoastal at a hundred miles an hour."

"But you'll go out with one," he said, and immediately regretted the comment.

She was quiet for a few moments, and then she answered in a low voice, "I'll marry one." She glanced over and caught his adoring gaze. Feeling exposed and foolish, he jerked his eyes back to the road and said nothing.

She rubbed her hand across the torn, rusty dashboard. "Nice truck," she said. "Your father's?"

"My Uncle Joe's. My father's dead. My mother, too. Car wreck on Alligator Alley." The words came out in a rush, as if he'd been waiting a very long time to tell her. And then he realized that in all the years he'd been coming to Paradiso Perduto, she'd never asked him any personal questions. How could that be? He was so wildly curious about her life that he hoarded every bit of information he could gather about her—where she went to school, how she spent her free time, her likes and dislikes. He thought of her as his friend, and yet she knew almost nothing about him. Was it because she just didn't give a damn?

"Did you know them?" she asked.

He nodded as he loosened the bow tie and pulled it off. "It happened when I was in first grade."

She flashed a sideways glance, as if she were wondering whether it was hard for him to talk about his parents.

He would have told her if she'd asked: No, it wasn't, not anymore. The accident had occurred so long ago, and so much had happened since then. He very infrequently dreamed about them—the same recurring dream about going fishing with his father and catching a pompano. He was eager to show off his catch to his mother, but by the time he reached home, the pompano had mysteriously disappeared. Neither of his parents was able to stop him from shedding bitter tears of grief over his loss. The dream always ended with his mother reaching out her arms to comfort him, but he invariably awakened before he could step into her hug.

Estella stubbed out her cigarette and flicked it through the open window. "I don't remember mine," she said. "I was adopted at two."

He was surprised by her statement. He'd always thought that Mrs. Dinsmoor was her aunt. He tried to imagine her as a small child, learning her way around the mansion. "Maybe that's better. You know, like being blind since birth. You don't miss what you've never known."

"Maybe." She shrugged, then lit another cigarette. "I like your jacket. Very chic."

He looked to see if she was teasing, but she seemed serious. "Thanks," he said, tempted to tell her the truth about its origins.

"My aunt has one just like it."

"Yeah." He smirked. "But it fits me better."

She burst out laughing, and he laughed with her, and after that the tension between them was broken. They chatted comfortably the rest of the way to Cortez, and he even got her giggling uncontrollably over his stories about some of the crazy characters who'd chartered Joe's fishing boat. He didn't feel nervous again until they pulled up in front of his building, and he became aware of how grubby and decrepit the place would look to her.

The Rhinebold twins were perched on the hood of a Camaro that was parked across the street. They were drinking beer straight out of the can, lip-synching to the Aerosmith CD on their portable player.

Jimmy cursed his bad luck and hustled Estella past them without a word or even a glance of acknowledgment. He should have known better than to give them the cold shoulder.

"Yo, James!" Gloria shouted as he crossed the street with Estella in tow. "You up for a blow job tonight?"

"The usual, babe. By the swings," Diane chimed in.

He didn't see them high-fiving each other behind his back, but he could hear them cackling all the way into his building.

Estella shot him a look that asked, *Friends of yours?*

"Local girls," he explained tersely. "Foolin' around."

"Sure," she said, smiling as she followed him up the stairs and into the apartment.

Joe had said that he and Maggie were going to Bradenton to catch a late movie and wouldn't be back until after midnight. Jimmy nevertheless took the precaution of checking the kitchen to make sure they were really out for the evening. He grabbed a couple of sodas out of the fridge and pointed at the light fixture. "Those moths flying around the lightbulb are from the 'thousand-wing' ceiling in Venice," he quipped. "Italy."

"Cute," she said and gave him a light punch on the arm.

She remembered, after so many years. He would have liked to ask her what else she remembered about his first visit to Paradiso Perduto, but he didn't want her to get distracted by a stroll down Memory Lane that could lead nowhere. So he swallowed his questions and watched her survey the apartment—the cheap, shabby furniture, the cracks in the walls that were way overdue for a paint job.

He had a sudden, sharp attack of serious doubts about the wisdom of bringing her home. As much as he wanted to spend time with her, he should have thought twice about letting her see how he lived, even if it had been her idea. And then he reminded himself of how *she* lived. Yes, her home was a mansion, filled with priceless objects of great beauty, but the place was in a state of utter disrepair.

Opening his bedroom door, he belatedly recalled the chaos he'd left behind. He scrambled ahead of her and scooped up the pieces of clothing piled all over the room. But it was impossible to create order out of anarchy in sixty seconds. He gestured at the mess and said, "I didn't expect . . ."

She shook her head and put her hand on his lips, to say, *It doesn't matter.* And why should it? She herself had grown up surrounded by clutter and disorder.

She walked over to his desk and wordlessly examined the paintings and sketches that were spread across it. "You still draw," she said finally.

He was both pleased and embarrassed to have her see his work. "Yeah. I sold one to a friend of my uncle's. A shark."

"You'll have to go to New York," she said, flipping through his sketchpad.

He hastily stuffed some pants into his dresser drawer, then turned to look at her. "New York?"

"It's the center of the art world," she said matter-of-factly. "You stay here, you'll wind up painting coconuts for tourists."

That assumed he planned to make a career out of art. The idea—apparently so simple and obvious to Estella—had never even occurred to him. He had no intention of joining the ranks of the hacks who haunted the docks, painting seascapes to sell on the cheap to Northerners with no taste. Joe's friend had liked his shark sketch so much that he'd pulled five ten-dollar bills out of his pocket and insisted on buying it. Jimmy would have given it to him for nothing if the guy hadn't already slapped the money down on the table.

Drawing was like breathing; he drew because he couldn't stop himself, because his fingers itched to pick up a pencil and reproduce his vision of what he saw around him. Hours could pass, the television might be blaring in the living room, Maggie could be yelling at him to come eat dinner, and he would hear nothing because he'd be so engrossed in whatever he working on at that moment.

But when he was done with school, he figured he'd go to work for Joe, or get a job hauling fishnets. What Estella didn't understand was that the closest a kid from Cortez could get to New York was in a movie theater.

He bent down to pick up a pile of clothes. When he stood up, he found her staring at the portrait he'd drawn of her.

"When did you do this?" she asked.

He dropped the clothes on his bed. "A while ago."

She stepped closer and pursed her lips. She said, finally, "I don't wear my hair like that anymore."

He shook his head. "No, but you should. I mean, it's—"

"You like it that way," she said, turning to stare at him.

The muscles in his stomach tightened with tension. He opened his mouth but was too nervous to speak. All he could do was nod in response.

"What else do you like?"

He didn't answer her question. Instead, he asked her a question, one he asked himself constantly. "How come . . . all these years . . .

I see you every week, and we never, you know, did anything together?''

She raised an eyebrow and reached in her bag for her cigarettes. ''Did anything?'' she said, removing the pack.

''Went out,'' he said, forcing himself to continue what he'd started. ''Saw a movie. Whatever.''

She took out a cigarette, then changed her mind and put it back in the pack. ''You never asked.''

He took a deep breath and stared at the strand of pearls around her neck because he couldn't meet her gaze. ''If I had?''

''I'm here, aren't I?'' she said quietly.

He'd waited so long to hear her say those words that he almost couldn't believe she meant what she was saying. He felt his knees buckling with the desire to hold her in his arms. He shoved aside the clothes on his bed and sat down heavily. Her bare legs were just inches away from his face. ''Are you . . . with anybody?'' he asked, breathing raggedly.

She tilted her head back and stroked the front of her neck. ''Right this second?''

''No,'' he said, gulping. Why did this have to be so difficult? He felt as if his head might explode if he didn't kiss her soon. ''I mean . . .'' He closed his eyes and tried to catch his breath. He thought, *I'm an idiot. I don't deserve her.*

"A boyfriend?" she said teasingly. Her leg brushed against his face. Startled, he glanced up at her, uncertain whether or not the contact had been deliberate. The touch of her bare skin made him feel feverish. He wanted to rip off his shirt, grab her, press his face against her thighs. He did none of those things, but instead sat still as a statue, watching her as she continued to stare at her portrait. Her leg caressed his cheek again, and this time he knew it was no accident.

Emboldened, he reached up and stroked the inside of her thigh, lightly running his fingers from her knee all the way up to where her leg disappeared beneath her dress.

She leaned into his hand but otherwise gave no sign that she was aware of his touch. "A steady boyfriend?" she said, continuing the conversation as if nothing were happening between them. "No."

"You could have anybody," he said, his fingers creeping a scant inch higher up on her leg.

She shook her head. "No rush. What about you?"

Before he had a chance to respond, she spread her legs, and he took that as permission to explore further. His hand disappeared beneath her skirt, moving agonizingly close to the V between her legs. His fingers grazed the edge of her underwear; he traced the curve of her silky-smooth thigh with his thumb. She rocked against his hand and closed her eyes, then opened them again and gazed unfocusedly at the picture above him.

"Me?" he whispered. "No."

"Why not?" she asked in a husky voice as his hand continued its exploration.

"I don't know," he said, and his voice, too, sounded low and shaky. "I haven't . . ."

She pressed herself into his fist and moved her hips closer to his face. "I know," she murmured. "I know."

The motion of her body felt like an invitation he would have been crazy to decline. He stood up abruptly, folded her into his arms, and kissed her. Her lips were as soft and full as he'd imagined them, her mouth was as sweet and enticing as he'd dreamed it would be. He pressed her against him and inhaled the scent of her hair and skin. She returned his kiss, and he felt the happiest he'd ever been in his life. She rubbed her lips against his and breathed a tiny, barely audible sigh of pleasure. And then, without any warning, she pulled away from him.

"What?" he said, reaching for her. "What's wrong?"

She caught her bottom lip between her teeth and gently pushed him away. "Nothing. It's late. What time is it?"

"Uh . . ." He glanced at his watch. "It's ten-thirty."

She straightened her skirt and frowned. "Really? I have to get home."

"Why?" he asked, grabbing her hand.

"I have a million things to do tonight," she said, as she shook herself free of him.

"Stay," he pleaded. He didn't expect them to make love. That possibility seemed too much to hope for. But he ached to hold her, to lie next to her and touch her. The thought of her leaving him now was unbearable. And yet, it was so predictable. She teased and mocked him mercilessly ever since the day they'd met. Tonight her teasing had reached a new level of sophistication—and cruelty.

She leaned forward and brushed her lips against his cheek. *"A bientot,"* she said.

He imagined—or was it merely wishful thinking?—a trace of regret in her voice. "I don't speak French," he reminded her.

Halfway out the door, she paused to take one last look at her portrait. *"Quel dommage,"* she said, and then she was gone.

No one was home when he arrived at the mansion the following week. He ventured as far as Mrs. Dinsmoor's bedroom, but there was no trace of her or Estella. Even the cat was gone. He'd been counting the hours until the next time he saw Estella. Perhaps, in his eagerness, he'd somehow mixed up the date. He searched the rest of the house, then hurried back outside and stumbled through the jungle of foliage that surrounded the mansion, calling out their names.

The afternoon was hot, the grounds silent except for the screeching birds overhead, the lizards scurrying through the underbrush, and the mosquitoes buzzing about his face. Jimmy brushed them away and shielded his eyes with his hand from the early summer sun. There was no trace of either one of them in the garden, so he continued deeper through the dense thicket of trees, slowly making his way toward the wall that surrounded the property.

He'd once, years earlier, explored the section of the estate that was bordered by the beach, and now he recalled seeing a metal door that had been cut in the wall on the ocean side of the mansion. It took him a few minutes to find the door, which was badly rusted and crisscrossed with thick creeping vines. Stepping closer, he saw that some of the vines were freshly ripped, as if the door had just recently been opened again after a very long time. He pushed open the door and found himself in a narrow, long, dark tunnel that was illuminated only by a bare bulb. The tile walls were glistening with slime, and the concrete floor was flooded with puddles of muddy water. A fresh ocean breeze wafted through, and the roar of the waves beckoned him forward as he gingerly picked his way between the puddles toward the faint gleam of light at the far end.

Eventually, he stepped out of the tunnel and onto a broad, sandy beach. The bright sun hit him like a floodlight that had just been switched on. It took a few seconds until his eyes readjusted and he spotted Mrs. Dinsmoor a few yards away. She was standing at the water's edge, decked out in a patent leather miniskirt and matching vest, and a silver Lurex stretch T-shirt. Cradling her beloved monster cat, she stared out at the horizon, the wind whipping her hair about her face.

She seemed to sense his presence even before he came up next to her. "Jimmy," she said, turning to greet him. "I need you here."

He jogged over to join her. "Have you seen Estella?" he asked.

Without any warning, Mrs. Dinsmoor shoved the cat into his arms. "It's time for Tabby's swim. Would you throw him in?"

The cat protested with an angry meow and clawed at Jimmy's face as it tried to wiggle out of his grasp. "In the water?" Jimmy asked dubiously.

"No, in the fire." Mrs. Dinsmoor's voice dripped sarcasm. "Go ahead," she urged. "He loves the sea. He's been such a bore, it'll wake him up. Go ahead. Just heave him in."

Jimmy had always thought that cats hated the water. But however Mrs. Dinsmoor felt about people, she seemed to truly love her monster pet. He shrugged, stepped closer to the water, and heaved the cat into the ocean. The animal landed in the surf on all fours, gave a leisurely stretch, and purred with obvious contentment.

His mind still focused on Estella, Jimmy was about to repeat his earlier question when Mrs. Dinsmoor turned to face him. "I never come here," she said, speaking so softly he had to strain to hear her words. "Never. Not in over twenty years. Do you know why?"

He'd become accustomed to her odd manner and behavior, but now, something about the intensity of her gaze made him uncomfortable. "Can't swim?" he joked, trying to defuse the tension.

She ignored him and continued speaking almost as if she were talking to herself. "Twenty-six years ago, I trusted . . . What kind of creature . . . ?" She stopped, knelt to scoop up a handful of sand, and watched it trickle through her open fingers. "I saved myself. I waited. You see? I saved myself for him. I was a virgin. Funny, huh? Those were the times. That's how I was raised."

Jimmy nodded politely, even as he wondered why she was confiding in him. She'd never told him anything about herself or her past, and it suddenly occurred to him that maybe she'd had too much to drink. Why else would she be sharing such personal information with him? And yet she didn't sound drunk. Just the opposite, in fact. But who was the "him" that she'd saved herself for?

A tear trickled down her cheek as she went on. "What kind of creature takes such a thing, such a gift? A trust. Who does this? Takes advantage of a forty-two-year-old woman? What kind of creature leaves this woman waiting like a fool, left alone, on a lonely beach with the sounds of music and laughter from her own wedding party . . . ?"

She almost seemed to be expecting an answer, but he was too busy struggling to make sense of what she was saying to offer a response. A wedding party? He watched the cat, its fur matted and waterlogged, swim to shore and stretch itself out on the sand. He tried to imagine Mrs. Dinsmoor as a bride, happy and hopeful and full of excitement about the future.

She covered her left breast with her hand, touching the spot beneath which beat her heart, just as she'd made him do so many years ago. "A man. A man does this," she said, paying no attention to the cat who was meowing piteously at her feet. "So men must pay. Am I right?" she demanded.

"I don't know, Mrs. Dinsmoor," he said, distracted again by thoughts of Estella.

As if she intuited the focus of his attention,

she quickly changed the subject. "Estella will make men weep."

"Where is she?" he asked, glad now that the conversation had shifted to his main concern.

But Mrs. Dinsmoor was off again on her own track. "Oh, yes. She'll break them. I taught her well. When she returns, she'll cut through them like a hot knife through butter," she said triumphantly.

"Returns?"

"From Europe." Mrs. Dinsmoor flashed him a brittle smile. "Oh, my sweet boy, didn't you know?"

"Know what?" he asked. He stared at Mrs. Dinsmoor. She was swaying back and forth, rotating her hips and shoulders, dancing to the music that only she could hear. He felt light-headed, as if he'd been out in the sun too long. He wanted to grab her arm and shake her until she stopped moving. And then he wanted her to laugh and reassure him that she was just joking about Estella.

She reached out to him instead, and touched his cheek in almost exactly the same spot where Estella had kissed him good-bye. She said, "Estella's left for school abroad. Switzerland for two years. Then Paris. She's gone. Didn't she say good-bye? I'm sure she meant to—"

He couldn't stay to hear more. If she were

lying, he had to find Estella quickly, hold her in his arms again, and admit how much he loved her. And if she were telling the truth, he had to get away from here, to put as much distance as possible between himself and Paradiso Perduto. If she were telling the truth—if she'd sent Estella to Europe for two or more years—he needed to leave behind forever Mrs. Dinsmoor, all his memories of Estella, all his hopes for their future.

"See you next week, dear," Mrs. Dinsmoor called as he sprinted down the beach toward the tunnel. He plunged through the opening in the wall, splashing through the puddles that he'd so carefully avoided just a few minutes earlier. He headed straight for the house, shouting Estella's name over and over again, running so hard and fast that by the time he reached the entrance hall, he was almost doubled over from a cramp in his side.

Stopping to recover his breath, he leaned against the marble fountain and looked up at the cascading stream of water. He remembered Estella at ten, leaning over to kiss his lips through the spray. She'd been playing with him then, teasing him, as usual. But when she'd kissed him in his bedroom after the party, he'd sensed that she was trying to tell him something. Now, as he felt the silence of the house closing in on him, he finally understood her message. She'd wanted him to know she was leaving. Her kiss had been her good-bye.

CHAPTER 6

Jimmy had paid his last visit to Paradiso Perduto. When he didn't show up the following week, Mrs. Dinsmoor didn't even bother phoning to find out why. He figured she knew the reason for his absence and was too proud to ask him to return. Besides, with Estella gone, who was there for him to dance with? He walked through the rest of his senior year like an automaton, skipped his prom and got falling-down drunk instead, and only showed up for graduation because Uncle Joe insisted on seeing him get his diploma.

He'd never planned to go to college, and he didn't have to worry about finding a job. He had one waiting for him, as Joe's first mate on the boat. He started the day after graduation, despite Joe's suggestion that he take it easy for a couple of weeks. The last thing in the world he wanted was a long stretch of free time with nothing to think about except Estella.

The sooner he started working, he figured, the sooner he'd put her out of his mind. But getting over her was much harder than he ever would have expected. She was like a drug, an addiction he had to battle in order to give up. Months went by before he could get through a day without stopping in mid-activity to wonder where she was at that moment, what she was doing, what she was thinking about, how she was feeling. He fantasized about getting her address in Switzerland from Mrs. Dinsmoor so he could write to her, but he could never bring himself to make the call.

A year went by, and then another, and then a third and a fourth. Jimmy's life settled into a routine that made sense to him unless he thought about it for too long. He still lived with Maggie and Joe because he couldn't come up with a good enough reason to move out and get his own place. He worked hard and, for the most part, liked what he was doing. Joe was good company, and Jimmy enjoyed pitting himself against the hammerhead sharks and other big fish that swam the waters off the Gulf Coast.

It took both muscles and a brain to capture hammerheads. They were mean and tough, and they didn't get caught without putting up a fight. They thrashed about so violently against the side of the boat, spraying blood and gore and seawater, that a man could easily lose his balance and fall overboard if he didn't take care. Hooking them was only half the battle. After Joe had slammed the eight-foot-long fish with a bangstick that contained a shotgun shell that exploded on contact, Jimmy had to haul the hammerhead over the side and onto the deck.

It was a man's job, and Jimmy had grown into it well before he'd reached his late twenties. He worked hard, and he played hard, too. He didn't have a steady girlfriend, but it wasn't for lack of interest among the young women he met in the neighborhood. He was widely considered to be the best-looking guy in Cortez: tan, fit, and well-muscled, with piercing blue eyes, strong cheekbones, and a sweetness that the girls found irresistible.

He was a particular favorite at the regular fish-fry parties thrown by the local fishermen who docked their boats at the Cortez pier. He was always good for a beer and a laugh, and a girl counted herself lucky if she scored a dance with Jimmy Bell, because he was easily the smoothest dancer in town. He was a good storyteller and knew how to tell a joke without ruining the punchline. But he rarely stayed around long enough to see anyone home. Instead, he would wander off alone to the end of the dock, where he would stare at the stars twinkling overhead, and at the vast expanse of the Gulf, shining like dark glass all the way to Mexico.

He'd given up painting, except what was necessary to fix up the boat when it needed more anti-barnacle cover or a fresh coat to the decks. Which was what he was doing in the middle of one scorching hot day when a blistering sun had sent most sensible people in search of shelter. He and Joe had hoisted the boat high and dry in its wooden brace, and he was splashing red paint across the hull, moving the brush to the blasting rhythms of James Brown.

He'd turned up the volume on the boom box so high that he didn't hear company coming until a shadow fell across the pier. He glanced up and was surprised to see, silhouetted by the sun, a tall, heavy-set man carrying a fancy leather briefcase. Joe stood alongside him in his usual jeans and T-shirt. But judging from the way the man was dressed, in an expensive-looking seersucker jacket and pants, Jimmy was pretty certain he wasn't looking to go fishing.

The man nodded at Jimmy, and Joe introduced him. "Jimmy, this is Jerry Ragno."

Jimmy rocked back on his heels, rubbed his palm on his shirt, and offered it to Ragno. What he got in return was a well-manicured hand and a firm grasp.

"Mr. Ragno's a lawyer in Miami," Joe explained.

"And New York. We have offices in Manhattan." Ragno pulled a white silk handkerchief out of his pocket and mopped beads of perspiration off his brow. Then he said, "Jimmy, tell me, do you still paint?"

Jimmy jerked his thumb in the direction of the boat. "Whenever they need it."

"I meant in the artistic sense," said Ragno.

Jimmy took his time standing up. He glanced sideways at Joe, who nodded, as if to say, *Go ahead, he's okay.* "I know what you meant," he said. "No. Not in years. Why?"

"I am empowered by my client to make your dreams come true," Ragno said.

"Really?" Jimmy asked warily. "What dreams?" He'd never believed in fairy tales, didn't even play the lottery. He'd learned through bitter experience with Mrs. Dinsmoor that most gifts came with long strings attached, and Ragno looked almost too slick to be trusted. "What client?"

Rather than answer the question, Ragno suggested they get out of the sun and have some lunch. He was buying, he said, and he had a taste for seafood. Jimmy caught Joe's wink and stifled a grin. He knew just the place.

The lawyer was sweating profusely by the time they arrived at the fish joint two blocks away that was frequented mostly by the local dockworkers and fishermen. Jimmy waved at the waitresses, both of whom he'd gone to school with, and chose a table overlooking the water. An umbrella furnished a circle of shade, but even the cool ocean breeze didn't provide much relief from the heat. Ragno gulped water, then took off his jacket and loosened his tie before he dug into a mound of steamed shrimp that just a few hours earlier had been swimming in the Gulf.

Jimmy and Joe exchanged amused glances as they watched the lawyer clumsily trying to extract the shrimp from their shells. Ragno waited until he was halfway through his meal to return to the subject at hand. "Have you ever shown your work?" he asked.

Before Jimmy had a chance to answer, Joe said, "They had Jimmy's painting up at Washington Federal Bank for—"

"That was seven, eight years ago," Jimmy broke in. "I told you, I gave it up. What's all this about, Mr. Ragno?"

Ragno wiped his hands, which were greasy from the side order of chips he'd ordered, and leaned forward across the table. "Would you like a show, a one-man show at the Thrall Gallery?"

Jimmy watched the lawyer take a long sip of beer. He wasn't sure he was hearing the man correctly. He knew about the Thrall Gallery, but the offer made no sense. "In New York?"

Ragno undid the clasp of his briefcase and pulled out a thin stack of papers. He pushed them toward Jimmy and said, "My client, Erica Thrall, wants to bring you to New York for a one-man show at her gallery."

"Why?" Jimmy demanded. He could feel his uncle, next to him, twitching with excitement. Turning to Joe, he snapped, "This is bullshit."

"Hear the man out," Joe begged, signalling the waitress for another round of beer.

A huge pelican landed on the railing behind Ragno and fluttered its wings. Startled, Ragno jerked his head away, then quickly recovered his composure and said, "Have you sent slides of your work to the Thrall?"

Jimmy shrugged. "Probably. I sent slides everywhere . . . when I was in high school."

Ragno jumped as the pelican snapped its beak at him. He shifted his chair away from the rail and continued on with his pitch. "Obviously, you made an impression," he said. He handed Jimmy an envelope. "A plane ticket to New York, and one thousand dollars. For incidentals. I'm sorry, it's all in hundreds."

Jimmy stared at the envelope. He thought back to the first time someone had thrust an envelope full of money into his hands. Although there was no way he could have known it at the time, he had ultimately paid too high a price for his compensation. He'd learned his lesson. He was not about to make get caught again in the same trap. He shoved the envelope back across the table. "The hundreds aren't the problem. I just don't paint anymore," he said.

To his credit, Joe didn't mention Ragno, neither when he was alone with Jimmy nor in front of Maggie. Jimmy appreciated his silence. He knew that Joe thought·he was nuts to turn down Ragno's proposition, and maybe his uncle was right. An all-expenses-paid trip to New York, along with the chance to exhibit at a major gallery, was every artist's dream. There was just one problem: he was no artist. He was a fisherman from a white trash town who liked to draw. Correction: who *used to* like to draw.

How and why would Erica Thrall be interested in his work? Even if he had sent her slides—and even if she had liked his unformed, adolescent attempt to evoke his world—why would she have waited until now to be in touch with him? You didn't need to be raised in Cortez to recognize that this deal smelled fishy.

And yet, he couldn't quite forget about Ragno and his offer. New York was the big time, the center of the art world. Estella had said so herself that night in his bedroom, the last time he'd seen her.

Estella. . . . Something clicked in his brain,

as if somebody had just flicked a switch, flooding a previously darkened room with light. He suddenly had an idea, and maybe it was a crazy one. But he had to pursue it, just in case he was right. Otherwise, he could be making the biggest mistake of his life.

He decided not to call ahead. He wanted to surprise her, to catch her off-guard. Or perhaps, if he was being honest with himself, he was afraid that if he called, she would tell him not to come.

He almost changed his mind when he pulled up in front of Paradiso Perduto. As he stared at the estate wall, overgrown with creeping branches and vines, he was assailed by a surge of memories he'd thought he'd permanently submerged. He forced himself out of the car and, as he walked through the gate, he caught a glimpse of his ten-year-old self, approaching the mansion in his brand-new suit from Sears.

He felt almost as nervous now, at twenty-seven, as he had felt that day. And nothing had changed—not the tangle of trees and bushes that lay between the gate and the house, nor the house itself, except that the deterioration had worsened over the course of the decade. He felt a pang of sadness as he passed the marble fountain and climbed the staircase, and though he could have found Mrs. Dinsmoor's room with his eyes closed, he wished that Estella were there, leading the way.

He had to smile when he reached her door. She was still listening to her favorite song, which he recognized now as the Ventures' version of "Besame Mucho." He knocked loudly and got no response. He tried again, but there was still no answer. He took a deep breath and opened the door, wondering what he would find in the room.

His worst terror—that Mrs. Dinsmoor would be lying dead on her bed—went unrealized. She was sitting at her dressing table, stroking Tabby the monster cat, who was nestled in her lap. She was staring at herself in an oversized magnifying makeup mirror that was lit by a circle of high-intensity bulbs, and though her back was to him, he saw that she had dyed her hair bright red.

"Mrs. Dinsmoor?" he said, wishing he'd thought to bring her flowers or a box of chocolates.

She didn't bother to turn around but said, "Is tea ready, Thomas?"

He stepped closer. "No, it's me, Jimmy."

After a long, uncomfortable pause, she swiveled around in her chair to face him. She squinted at him through the gloom but didn't speak. The song came to an end, but still she was quiet.

He knew it was up to him to break the silence he'd imposed between them so many years ago. "I came . . ." he said, and then he stopped. How to explain why he'd come, when he hadn't explained why he'd stayed away?

"Looking for Estella," she said finally. "I know. That hook is in deep, isn't it, dear?"

She was right, of course, though it took her saying the words aloud to make him see what was so obvious. But his visit wasn't only about Estella. "I came to ask you a question," he said quietly.

"I see," she said, and there was no missing the edge in her voice. "After nearly ten years without a visit. Without a word. You've come to interrogate me. How thoughtful."

She was right again, and there was nothing for him to say except, "I'm sorry. Things happened."

His apology seemed to work. Her waxy features creased in a broad smile and she nodded agreeably. "I know what happened. The love of your life left you. It hurts, doesn't it? Come." She pointed at him with her long, bony index finger, the nail of which was painted bright yellow. "Come closer."

He picked his way through the jumble of belongings strewn across the floor to stand beside her. She hadn't stopped petting Tabby since he'd walked into the room, and he was shocked to see that a patch of fur had been worn away by her caresses. But a far worse shock awaited him when he looked more closely. The cat was dead.

He was about to ask when and how it had happened. Then he decided he would rather not know.

Mrs. Dinsmoor patted her hair with her free hand. "I've gone red."

"I noticed," he said and tried not to stare at the dead cat in her lap, which was giving off a more than slightly unpleasant smell. "It's nice."

She reached out, grabbed his hand, and pulled him closer. "And look at you," she murmured, stroking his face. "All grown up. A man."

He gently freed himself from her grasp and knelt beside her chair. He'd thought a lot about the best way to ask her what he needed to know, then decided the direct approach was best. But now, face-to-face with her after so many years, acting on his intention was more difficult than he'd expected. "Mrs. Dinsmoor, a lawyer, a man named Ragno, came to see me," he began, groping for the right words.

"The spider." She nodded.

"Do you know him?" he asked, surprised that she would admit so quickly to being his patron.

" 'Ragno' means spider in Italian," she said. "You must learn other languages, James."

She was so good at playing mind games. But he'd learned a thing or two since he was a kid, totally at her mercy. "This lawyer, Ragno, he says he represents an art gallery owner in New York. They want to show my work."

She raised a well-plucked eyebrow, then conceded, "You *can* draw. Can't dance worth a shit, but you can draw."

"What I want to ask you . . ." He sighed, stood up, and put a few feet of distance between them. "Did you . . . do you know anything about this?"

She dropped her head, hiding her face behind her hair so that he wasn't able to read her expression. Her response, when it finally came, ignored his question, yet told him exactly what he'd hoped to hear.

"Estella is in New York."

He managed, somehow, not to let his excitement show. He felt as if Mrs. Dinsmoor already had an unfair advantage over him, and he didn't want to add to her ammunition. "I doubt our paths would cross," he said flatly.

"So you're going?"

"Do you think I should?" he asked, surprised to discover he truly was interested in her opinion.

Her gaze shifted from him to the ruined garden beyond the mansion, visible through the window. "I remember I watched you from this very window. A scared little mouse scurrying across my garden and through my front door," she said. She turned her head and stared directly into his eyes. "And now, another door opens. What will our mouse do?"

He hated her. She was a cruel, manipulative woman. But he loved her, too. He'd never realized that until now. For better or worse, she'd played a role in creating the person he'd become. He was willing to bet she was still meddling in his life by bankrolling his trip to New York. Because he was going, he realized. He couldn't *not* go. The possibility that he might see Estella again was too tantalizing an opportunity to forego. The art show was secondarily important. He didn't have much to show Erica Thrall. But he had plenty to say to Estella.

"Thanks for your time," he said politely. "I have to go."

"The Gershwins lived in New York," she told him, as if he should know who the Gershwins were.

"Really?"

"Jews," she said dismissively.

She was a snob and a bigot. He understood now what he couldn't have understood as a child. She was an old lady, and she couldn't help herself. The habit was too ingrained. He wondered how many of her prejudices Estella had adopted as her own. Eager to get away from her, he backed toward the door.

"I expect an invitation," she said.

"Sorry?"

"To your show. Your opening."

"Of course," he said, though he couldn't imagine her ever leaving Paradiso Perduto.

"And one for Tabby." She raised the dead cat's paw to her lips.

He fled the room, closing the door firmly behind him.

Leaving Cortez was much easier than he could have guessed. His friends threw him a farewell party on the beach where prodigious quantities of beer were consumed, along with large amounts of steamed shrimps and clams. There was lots of loud music and dancing, as well as good-natured toasting and roasting of the guest of honor. The party lasted until the cops showed up just before sunrise, and Jimmy woke up twelve hours later with a bad hangover and a more than sneaking suspicion that he'd done well to take Ragno up on his offer.

The morning of his flight, before Maggie went off to her part-time cashier's job at the grocery store, she gave him a quick peck on the cheek and told him to behave himself. The only hard part was saying good-bye to his uncle, who drove him to the airport. Joe seemed determined to keep the conversation light all the way to Tampa. He turned on the radio, which was tuned as usual to the country-western station, and sang along with Tammy Wynette, Tanya Tucker, and Clint Black. Between songs, he delivered a detailed monologue about his plans to refurbish the boat, then broke off abruptly as if it had just hit him that Jimmy wouldn't be around for the next few months to crew for him.

After they pulled up in front of the terminal, he stood by awkwardly as Jimmy pulled his bags out of the back of the truck. "What kind of equipment you flyin'?" he asked, jingling the change in his pockets.

"What?"

"They got you in a wide-body? A 767?"

Jimmy checked his ticket, then shrugged. "No idea. As long as it stays up there."

A couple with two children and an improbable amount of luggage pushed between them and headed for the terminal entrance. Joe checked his watch and cleared his throat. He said, "Well, I guess you better—"

"What if I can't do it?" Jimmy said, unexpectedly ambushed by a severe attack of nerves. He felt like a kid, going off to his first day of school, scared to let go of all that was known and familiar. "I mean, what if I get up there, and I can't—?"

Joe put his hand on Jimmy's shoulder. "There is nothing harder than being given your chance," he said.

Jimmy took a long last look at his uncle, seeing the wrinkles around his eyes and mouth, the sunbeaten creases in his forehead. They were related by marriage, not blood, but Joe had been like a father—and sometimes a mother—to him. He wished he could think of a way to thank him for all that he'd done. But anything he might say would only embarrass them both, so he smiled his gratitude and settled for, "I'll call you when I get up there."

Joe nodded. "I'll be here," he said and enveloped Jimmy in a hug.

Jimmy picked up his bags and walked towards the terminal. He turned back just as the electric doors swung open. Joe was still there, leaning against the side of the truck. The last thing Jimmy saw before the doors closed was Joe's smile and his unmistakable thumbs-up salute.

Nothing he'd ever experienced could have prepared him for New York. The first hurdle he encountered was finding his way into Manhattan from LaGuardia Airport. Jerry Ragno had given him a quick course in New York geography: The airport, he'd explained, was located in the borough of Queens, a sprawling suburb that was connected to Manhattan by several bridges and a tunnel. The cheapest mode of transportation was a bus-and-subway combination that would deliver him to a stop only a short walk away from the Thrall Gallery in midtown.

What Ragno hadn't bothered to mention was how crowded and uncomfortable the subway could be, especially for someone hauling a suitcase, a duffel bag, and a knapsack. He stood jammed sideways against a pole, trying to keep his balance as the train racketed and lurched through the underground darkness. All the windows were tightly shut, and there hardly seemed enough air to breathe. At each successive station, oncoming passengers stumbled over his luggage and loudly vented their displeasure with angry words and dirty looks. His muttered apologies hardly seemed to placate them, so he finally gave up and tried to fix his features in the same blank disinterested expression worn by his fellow travellers.

Ragno had instructed him to get off at the Fifth Avenue stop. He struggled up the station stairs and discovered that a torrential storm had erupted during the hour or so since he'd left LaGuardia. Sheets of rain cascaded from the overhang, and pools of water covered the pavement. A brisk wind sent sheets of newspaper whipping past his face, and a discarded soda can skittered across the sidewalk. People rushed by, heedlessly jostling him with their umbrellas as if he were invisible.

To his right was a low stone wall, and beyond that, an expanse of green lawn and trees that he guessed was Central Park. Across the street, on Fifth Avenue, a row of soaring skyscrapers glowed against the early evening sky. Cars, buses, and taxis crawled through the gloomy dusk, honking their horns in a noisy cacophony that no one seemed to mind but him.

He straddled his luggage, pulled up the hood of his sweatshirt, and buttoned up his worn leather jacket. He rechecked Ragno's directions and studied the street signs. Then, juggling his equipment, he lowered his head to keep the rain out of his eyes and hustled through the storm toward what he hoped was his destination.

He was thoroughly drenched and shivering by the time he reached the gallery, which occupied a street-level space between Madison and Park avenues and was fronted with floor-to-ceiling windows. Through the glass, he could see people milling about, chatting in small groups and gazing at the paintings hung on the stark white walls. He watched as several uniformed waiters moved about the room carrying trays of food and wine that they offered to the guests.

A small hand-lettered sign on the door read, "Exhibit opening tonight. Attendance by invitation only." He pulled the hood off his head, tried to shake some of the rain from his jacket, and pushed open the door.

The entrance was blocked by a round table presided over by three beautiful, model-thin young women, dressed in short black dresses that accentuated their perfectly sculpted bodies.

One of the women had long red hair that hung in thick curly ringlets around her face; the other two had sleek short cuts that looked as if they'd been hand-painted onto their heads. All three looked at Jimmy, as he stood dripping water on the table, as if he were a bum who had stumbled in off the street.

The red-haired woman picked up a piece of paper and made a big show of moving it away from him. "Yes?" she said coldly.

He shifted from one foot to the other and wished he didn't care that he was dressed in jeans and water-logged sneakers instead of the stylish suits that the other men were wearing. "I just got in," he said, feeling like a fool for showing up unannounced. "I'm supposed to see Mrs. Thrall."

The woman in the middle tapped her red-polished fingernail against the table top. "Name?" she asked.

"Bell. Jimmy," he said. He heard himself and didn't like how he sounded. Like a kid from the sticks. Wet behind the ears and totally out of his class. His name alone was a dead giveaway. Who had ever heard of an artist named Jimmy? He made a quick decision, reconfigured his identity, and said, "James Bell. I doubt I'm on any list. I'm just supposed to—"

"No," the red-haired woman interrupted

him, scanning her list. "You're not. I'm sorry."

"She's expecting me. She'll want to see me."

The woman sighed and pursed her lips. She turned to the young woman seated on the end and said, "Marci?"

Marci groaned with evident annoyance. She shook her head as she stood up. He followed her with his eyes as she glided toward the back of the gallery.

"Would you mind?" the red-haired woman said, motioning him away from the table as more party guests came through the door.

He backed away from the entrance and stepped outside into the rain, which was still coming down heavily. Peering through the window, he watched the woman named Marci ease her way past the well-dressed throng until she found another, equally thin woman in a tightly fitted white suit and a helmetlike, raven-black hairdo. The woman was engrossed in a lively conversation with a handsome older man and a much younger and extremely glamorous woman. Marci waited until the white-suited woman stopped talking, then tapped her on the arm and whispered something in her ear.

The white-suited woman, whom he guessed was Erica Thrall, nodded at Marci and glanced in his direction. He waved at her. In return, he got a chilly smile and a vague look of recognition. Then she mouthed something at Marci and went back to her conversation.

He reminded himself that he was here by her personal invitation, extended through Ragno. So maybe he wasn't wearing the right kind of clothes, and he didn't exactly look like the rich folks inside. But he was about to become one of Erica Thrall's artists, soon to have his own exhibition, maybe even a fancy opening night party just like this one. Eager to meet her, he picked up his duffel bag and slung it over his shoulder.

He heard a loud moan at the same instant that he felt the duffel make contact with something solid. Turning, he saw that the bag had slammed into the face of one of the guests. The man slid to the ground and landed on his behind.

Jimmy quickly knelt beside him. "Jesus! I'm sorry."

Blood was gushing out of the man's nose, and he winced as he checked it for damage. Dazed, he brushed a strand of blond hair out of his eyes and stared up at Jimmy, as if trying to make sense of what had just happened to him.

"I know you," Jimmy said, stunned to discover a familiar face here in the middle of New York. A familiar face that he'd unwittingly assaulted, no less.

The man blinked, trying to place him.

"Shit!" he said. "You were the jerk with Estella. Back in Sarasota!" He moaned again and struggled to his feet, still holding his nose.

"Right. Sorry about this."

The man gave him a lopsided grin. "Fuck it. I'm Owen Tulp," he said. He pulled a handkerchief out of his pocket, twisted into a spiral, and jammed it into his nostril to staunch the flow of blood.

"James Bell," Jimmy said.

Owen Tulp chuckled weakly. "Well, nice 'bumping' into you again." He walked through the gallery door, stopping to give Marci, who had just reappeared, a big hug. As Jimmy tried to follow him inside, the young woman blocked his way and said, "She'd like you to come by tomorrow."

"Oh." He tried to hide his disappointment as he suddenly realized how cold and hungry and tired he was after the long day of travel. The scene inside the gallery looked so warm and inviting. He asked Marci, "Did she say . . . ?" He felt too discouraged to complete the sentence.

"She said, 'Welcome to New York.' "

A thousand dollars, Ragno had told him, might sound like a great deal of money. But this was New York, where a hotel could easily set him back a hundred and fifty dollars a night, and a hamburger could cost seven bucks without a side of fries or even a slice of cheese melted on top. The lawyer had warned that if he weren't careful, the money could trickle through his fingers so fast that he'd be back in Cortez before he'd had a chance to lose his tan.

Mindful of Ragno's cautionary words, Jimmy decided to forego a taxi and walk across town through the pouring rain to the hotel on Eighth Avenue and Forty-second Street that one of his buddies had recommended. His friend, who'd spent a week in New York, had described the Carter Hotel as the kind of place where the guy behind the front desk was more interested in watching girls with big breasts dance naked on cable TV than in telling you how to get to the Empire State Building. "You want to watch your wallet," his friend had advised him.

Jimmy figured that his years of experience battling sharks and barracudas—not to mention Maggie—had prepared him for just about anything he might meet up with in New York. Still, he almost jumped out of his skin when he stopped at a corner to wait for the light to change and heard a voice behind him shout, "You're fucking a dead man!"

He turned and saw a man, dressed in a suit with a briefcase at his feet, standing at a pay-phone, raving into the receiver.

"No! No, you listen!" the man yelled. "You are fucking a dead man. . . . Yes, that's—

You know how I know? Because I'm gonna kill the motherfucker!''

The man listened a moment to the person on the other end, opened his mouth to speak, then screamed, "Shit!" He glanced around and noticed Jimmy. "Hey!" he called.

"Sorry?" Jimmy said, wiping the rain from his face.

"You got change for a dollar?"

The light had just turned green, and Jimmy could see the hotel's sign across the street. He was soaked to the bone and completely exhausted. All he wanted was to be someplace warm and dry. But the man sounded so distressed that it was hard to ignore him. He sighed as he put down his bags and dug in his pocket for coins. He was counting out a dollar when a bicycle ridden by a man in a yellow slicker rocketed around the corner and slammed into his bags, sending them skidding into the flooded street. The biker swerved, recovered his balance, and spat a string of curses at Jimmy before he vanished down the block as quickly as he'd appeared.

He'd left his mark, however, on Jimmy's duffel bag. The bag had ripped open, and Jimmy's belongings had spilled out across Forty-second Street. His roll of paintings—his life's work which he's so painstakingly packed to show Erica Thrall—was now scattered all over the road. He dived into the street, darting left and right as he snatched up the canvases before they were destroyed beneath the wheels of the oncoming traffic. He stooped to pick up the last one and staggered back to the curb.

"Well?" The man at the phone was still waiting for his change.

Jimmy flipped him a quarter. *Welcome to New York,* he thought. Catching sharks was a day at the beach compared to surviving in the Big Apple.

CHAPTER 7

His reception the next morning at the Thrall
Gallery was not at all what he'd expected. One
of the thin young women from the night before
silently ushered him into Erica Thrall's starkly
decorated, all-white office. The gallery owner
was seated behind a very large and very modern white desk, talking French into a sleekly
designed cordless phone. A pair of glasses was
pushed up onto her head, and diamond earrings
glowed in her earlobes. Several thick gold
bracelets jangled on her arm as she kept
straightening the same pile of perfectly aligned
papers on her otherwise spotless desk.

Owen Tulp was sitting in one of the two
chairs across from her. He smiled when Jimmy
walked into the room and pointed to his
slightly swollen nose. Owen, it turned out,
worked at the gallery.

After what felt like an interminable wait, Erica Thrall finished her phone call. Without wasting a moment on conversational niceties, she immediately turned her attention to inspecting Jimmy's works.

She glared at the top canvas, an oil painting of Joe's rusty truck. "Nope." She scornfully dismissed it, then thumbed through the rest of the stack as Owen peered over her shoulder. "No," she said, shaking her head at one after another of what he considered to be his best pieces. "No. Never."

Whatever promises Erica Thrall might have made to Mrs. Dinsmoor, if indeed the old lady was his patron, she seemed to have forgotten her commitment.

Too chagrined to conceal his disappointment, Jimmy said, "I don't understand."

"They're nice paintings. Safe as milk." Erica Thrall grimaced. "Have you thought of commercial art, darling?"

"There's no danger," Owen said. "It's the end of the millennium, for Christ's sake."

Danger? The millennium? Jimmy shook his head. What the heck was Owen talking about? Danger was a wounded shark coming at you when your bangstick didn't work. Danger was getting caught in your boat on open water in the middle of a lightning storm. Danger was a hurricane bearing down on the coast without adequate warning.

"What's this?" Erica Thrall said suddenly. She stared at a painting he'd done of the Rhinebold sisters when they were in high school. The canvas, a casualty of last night's accident, was stained and cracked. Chunks of oil paint were missing, and a tire tread rumpled the upper left corner.

"Oh shit." Jimmy grabbed for it. "This shouldn't be—"

"It's marvelous," Erica Thrall said.

"—At the back of the pile," Jimmy improvised. "I meant to start with it."

She held it up so Owen could see it. "Excellent," he agreed.

"It's . . ." Jimmy cast about for a way to explain the divergence between his two styles. "I've been working on this new technique for quite—"

"Lovely." Erica Thrall nodded. "Do you have any others?"

"Others?"

"Like this. Any more like this?" she asked impatiently.

He grabbed the rest of the canvases and flipped through them.

"I'll only want the portraits," she said. The phone rang. "Hang on . . ." She grabbed the cordless. "*Liebchen! Gut morgen!* Are you still holding the Picasso? The red-and-green one?"

Dammit! There was nothing else that would

pass her critical test. So much for his brilliant artistic career. Ah, well, he consoled himself, he loved fishing, and from what little he'd seen so far, living in New York was no great shakes. He would stay until his money ran out, try to find Estella, maybe even persuade her to come back with him to Cortez. He slumped in his chair and steeled himself to give Erica Thrall the bad news.

"Because I think I have someone interested," she told the person on the other end.

Owen caught his eye and mouthed, *Don't worry.*

"I can't say right now," she continued. "Just the Picasso. Talk to—" She nodded, then went on, *"Fabelhaft. Danke."* She hung up and turned back to him expectantly. "I'm sorry. Where were we?"

He shook his head. "There are no other portraits."

She glanced at Owen and shrugged, as if to say, What am I supposed to do? Then she leaned across the desk and said, not unkindly, "Look, darling, it's a personal thing. Taste. Somebody else might love them all. This painting is in the direction my clients will respond. Give me, say, fifteen more portraits in that style, I think we could help you. I'll understand completely if you want to work with another gallery."

But no other gallery owner had expressed

interest in his work. Something didn't add up here. He remembered exactly what Ragno had said: "My client, Erica Thrall, wants to bring you to New York for a one-man show at her gallery." Didn't she have an obligation to make good on her commitment?

"So?" she prompted him.

He'd faced down all kinds of risks, including a convict on the run, in his twenty-seven years. Yet something about Erica Thrall scared him more than any of the life-threatening situations in which he'd found himself. She felt like more of a different species than any fish he'd ever laid eyes on. He wanted to remind her of her promise, but because she scared him, all he said was, "Fifteen new paintings could take months."

She shrugged. "Whatever you need. I'm pretty booked right now, anyhow. Who knows? Maybe you'll get inspired." The phone rang again. "Think about it. Get back to me when you—"

"I'll do it," he said, surprising himself. "I can do it."

"Good." She said to Owen, "Get a contract from Marci." Turning back to Jimmy, she said, "Call me when you're ready." She reached for the phone. The meeting was over.

Reality hit as soon as he left the gallery. Jimmy stormed down Fifty-seventh Street with no idea of where he was going and what he planned to do. The storm from the previous evening had passed, and the sun was shining. The sidewalk was so crowded with pedestrians that it took him a minute to notice that Owen had caught up with him. He was glad to have the company, because he had plenty to say, and Owen was the only person he knew in New York City.

"Who the fuck is she?" he demanded of his new friend. "So, what, she jerks me up here for nothing? 'Taste, darling.' Taste this!" He gestured rudely with his finger and doubled his pace.

"Where are you going now?" Owen asked, panting as he hurried to keep up.

Jimmy glowered at Owen. "I don't know. I thought I'd take in a show. Hit a few clubs." Then, his bravado fading, he shrugged and admitted, "I'm going home."

"You go back, you'll never get up here again. You have to stay," Owen insisted.

Jimmy laughed bitterly. Easy for Owen to say. His family had money, he had a job, he had the right kind of clothes and connections. "You gonna support me?"

Owen clapped him on the back. "Maybe. I can get you decent money. One call. Take you a few weeks to do. But it's just between us. I'd rather Thrall doesn't know."

A couple, holding hands, bumped into Jimmy as he stopped short to stare at Owen.

The man threw him a dirty look and seemed eager to start a fight, but the woman tugged at his arm and pulled him away. Jimmy pushed Owen out of the flow of traffic and said, "About what?"

"A portrait. I can get you money to paint a portrait."

Although Jimmy could think of no logical reason why he should trust Owen Tulp, he nevertheless believed Owen would deliver on his pledge to find him work. Perhaps it was desperation that drove him to put his faith in a near-total stranger. Or perhaps it was their shared link to Estella. But the fact of the matter was, he wanted to stay in New York, at least long enough to prove himself to Erica Thrall. She had thrown up a challenge, and he had never backed away from a dare. He wanted to prove himself to her. He wanted to prove himself to Estella. And maybe, if he were lucky, Owen would lead him to her.

In the meantime, while he waited to hear from Owen, he decided to play tourist. He spent the next few days exploring as much as he could cover of the city: the Upper East Side with all its old money and chi-chi boutiques; SoHo, the hip downtown neighborhood where black jeans and a leather jacket seemed to be required garb for all those in search of cutting-edge art and fashion; the Times Square theater district with its bright lights and frenzied energy; the Empire State Building, the Statue of Liberty, and Central Park, where he spent several blissful hours sketching a panoramic view of the city's skyline from a surprisingly peaceful patch of green lawn called the Sheep Meadow. Best of all were the museums—the Metropolitan, the Modern, and the Guggenheim—where he was both inspired and discouraged by the roomfuls of masterpieces whose beauty was beyond anything he could have imagined.

He had just returned from the Met when Owen called to tell him he had an appointment the following evening with a man named Walter Plane. Walter, Owen said, fancied himself a "patron of the arts," and he had enough money to support an entire army of artists. He'd also spent a lot of winters in Florida and was likely to be particularly sympathetic to someone trying to escape what Plane liked to describe as "that backwater Southern mentality."

Jimmy was supposed to meet Plane at the Metropolitan Club on East Sixtieth Street. He could find him in the gym, where he would have just finished his workout. Yes, said Owen, it was an odd place to meet. But Plane was an odd sort of fellow. Oh yes, and one more thing, what a coincidence. Plane happened to be dating their mutual friend, Estella Dinsmoor.

The gym was equipped with a dazzling display of state-of-the-art bodybuilding machines, but Walter Plane was nowhere to be found among the men working out there. Jimmy checked the locker room under the watchful supervision of a uniformed employee, then eventually found him in the Olympic-sized pool, where he was swimming laps. Plane looked to be in his mid-forties, and from what Jimmy could see as he churned through the water with his butterfly stroke, he was a powerful, well-built man with broad, muscular shoulders.

Their appointment had been set for seven o'clock. But it was closer to seven-thirty when Plane completed his swim and hoisted himself out of the pool, splashing water all over Jimmy's shoes in the process. A club attendant hurried over to drape an oversized towel across Plane's shoulders, then just as quickly disappeared. Plane brushed back his thinning hair and stared at Jimmy with undisguised curiosity.

"You look like an artist," he said finally.

Jimmy had the impression that Plane wasn't paying him a compliment. He opened his mouth to introduce himself. "I—"

"Have Edward lend you a jacket and meet me in the dining room," Plane said curtly and walked past him toward the locker room.

"Right," Jimmy said to the empty space where Plane had stood just a second ago. But who was Edward? And why did he need a jacket?

By the time he tracked down Edward, who turned out to be the assistant manager of the dining room, and exchanged his leather jacket for a navy suit jacket that was too short in the sleeves ("Because it's our dress code, sir," Edward had stiffly explained), Walter Plane was already seated in the club's lavishly decorated dining room. Although the room was more than half full, people were speaking in such low, quiet tones that as Jimmy followed Edward across the plush carpeting to Plane's table, he forced himself to stifle a sneeze, so as not to disturb the hushed atmosphere.

But he couldn't stop himself from gaping at the heavy ivory drapes, tied back with red velvet ropes, that hung from the windows, and the matching ivory cloths that covered the tables, which were set with delicate gold-trimmed china, sparkling silverware, and several sizes of crystal goblets next to each plate. Immense oil paintings, all of which had a nautical theme, hung on the walls, and a glittering chandelier was suspended from the ceiling. Flickering candles set in ornate sconces added to the illusion that diners had stepped into the previous century.

Owen had told him that Plane had all but agreed to commission a portrait of himself, that all he wanted was to meet Jimmy to make sure he wouldn't hate him during the however-many hours it would take to do the preliminary sketches. There was no need to be nervous, Owen had assured Jimmy. Plane was virtually ready to sign on the dotted line.

Three days earlier, fresh off the plane, he might have been able to take Owen's advice. But in the short time he'd spent in New York, he'd been smitten by its charms. Walking the streets, he'd felt the city's pulse, heard the hum of its energy, tasted its varied flavors. He wanted to stay, to savor everything it had to offer. He could always go back to Cortez. The job on Joe's boat came with a lifetime guar-antee. Plane represented his chance to try on a different life, to realize the boyhood dream he'd never known was his until now.

He couldn't help but be nervous as he ap-proached Plane's table. But Owen hadn't men-tioned—perhaps he hadn't known until it was too late to warn him—that he and Plane would not be dining alone. Jimmy was the last to join the group, which included Owen; Lois Marx, a middle-aged woman with a face like a horse and a laugh to match; and a beautiful girl named Estella who looked like a princess and greeted him as if he were the long-lost friend she'd been searching for all her life.

By luck or design, the only empty chair was directly next to hers, and it took all his self-control not to reach over and grab her hand. The time she'd spent in Europe had left its mark on her. In the ten years since he'd seen her, she had been transformed from a beautiful girl into a young woman of exquisite style and grace. She was exactly the same, and she was totally different. But he would have to wait to get reacquainted with her, because Walter Plane wanted to tell a story, and he was obviously used to having his way.

He had ordered red wine for the table, and as he spoke, a waiter filled a glass for Jimmy without asking what he wanted to drink.

"A long time ago, there lived two brilliant artists," Plane began. "True geniuses, both of them. One day, one of the artists was out in the forest painting, and he saw a little dog. Crying and lost."

"A puppy?" Owen asked.

"Please." Plane frowned at the interruption. A chastened Owen grabbed for his wine and gulped down half the glass. "So the artist scoops up the little dog," Plane continued, "and takes it back into town to find its rightful owner. Who turned out to be the prince of the entire kingdom."

He caught Jimmy's gaze and winked. "The artist hands the grateful prince back his dog. That artist's name is Michelangelo. The other artist was never heard from again."

Lois clapped her hands and Owen chuckled appreciatively. Plane glanced at Estella, who seemed to be transfixed by the paintings on the wall opposite her. Jimmy watched as Plane reached over and touched her bare arm. Estella met his gaze and smiled, but Jimmy saw from her eyes that she was as unamused by the story as he was.

"That's so true, Walter." Lois jumped in to break the awkward silence. "I remember de Kooning once told me—"

"Enough, Lois. We've all heard your de Kooning stories," Owen said wearily.

Jimmy pulled out his pack of cigarettes and saw that there was only one left. He was about to light up when he noticed Estella staring at it. "You want?" he offered.

She shook her head. "It's your last one."

"Take it," he said. The cigarette was the least of it. Didn't she know he was willing to give her his life?

He leaned over to light it for her, and as he struck the match, she cupped her hands around his. The gesture was so ordinary, yet so private that he felt as if the air between them was charged with electricity.

She inhaled deeply, then passed it back to him. She gave no sign of having seen Plane's scowl as he watched their interaction. He snapped his fingers to summon the waiter and pointed to the empty package. His message was clear: Estella would smoke her own damn cigarette, if he had anything to say about it. Did he? Jimmy wondered. Were they together? Or did their relationship exist only in Plane's imagination?

Plane turned to him and said, "You're from Florida, too?"

He nodded.

"Isn't that wild?" Owen chimed in.

"I spent too many winters as a kid in Palm Beach," Plane growled.

"Jimmy and I were childhood . . ." Estella smiled at Jimmy. "What exactly were we? I guess you were my first love."

"If you say so," he said, hoping he sounded calmer than he felt. He'd waited forever to hear her say those words. There was so much he wanted to ask and tell her. He needed to be alone with her, away from all these people. Away from Walter Plane, who was staring at Estella as if he owned her.

Estella seemed unaware of Plane's displeasure. Her gaze still fixed on Jimmy, she said, "He drew a portrait of me when I was ten years old. It was so beautiful."

"I sat for a portrait once. Electric experience," Lois declared.

"Great, you slept with de Kooning," Owen said. "Can we get on with our lives?"

Jimmy riveted his eyes on Estella. He didn't

care that he might be throwing away his chance to work for Plane, and with it the opportunity to have a career in New York. "I want to paint you again," he said.

"You do?" Estella's question felt like a caress.

"I'd like to paint your portrait."

She shifted slightly in her chair and turned to ask Plane, "What do you think, love?"

A slap across the face could not have stunned or hurt him more than the pain he experienced, hearing her address Plane so intimately.

Lois, who was too stuck on Owen's last comment to bother tuning in to the rest of the conversation, suddenly trumpeted, "I *never* slept with Willy!"

She may as well have been speaking to herself. All eyes, including Owen's, were on Plane. He slowly sipped his wine, then said, "That depends. Do you charge by the inch or by the hour?"

Owen, caught up in the role of Plane's fawning toady, supplied a hearty chuckle. Estella's expression showed no discernible emotion.

Baffled by Plane's question, Jimmy said, "What?"

Plane picked up a breadstick and snapped it in half. "Do you price your art by the size—you know, the square footage—or by the time it takes to make?"

Owen laughed again, more loudly, and was joined this time by Lois. Estella smiled indulgently at Plane. Jimmy tried to look amused, but he could barely manage to hide his hurt and anger.

He endured the rest of dinner on automatic pilot, responding politely whenever anyone asked him a question, nodding and smiling when it seemed appropriate. But beneath his mask of amiability, he was seething with rage and confusion. Estella was up to her old tricks. Nothing had changed between them. She had set him up for the punch and enjoyed watching him take it on the nose.

He remembered what Mrs. Dinsmoor had told him the day he'd found her on the beach: "Estella will make men weep." But not Jimmy Bell. He wasn't about to shed any tears over her. He didn't care what happened with Walter Plane. Screw Plane, and screw her, too.

He couldn't get away from them fast enough. When Plane suggested an after-dinner cognac in the club's living room, he said, no, thanks, he'd already made other plans. He stomped out of the club, concocting elaborate, improbable schemes to punish Plane—for what, he wasn't altogether clear. As for Estella, he'd buried his feelings for her before. He could bury them again, this time so deeply that they would never, ever resurface to torment and haunt him.

He was halfway down the block before he heard someone calling to him, "Sir! Excuse me, sir!" He looked around and saw one of the waiters from the dining room chasing after him. "What do you want?" he demanded when the man got closer.

"The jacket, sir?" the waiter said.

The final indignity: he yanked off the jacket, traded it for his own leather one, and stalked off into the night.

He was deep in sleep, dreaming of Estella. She was dancing with him on the beach at sunset. The sky was a cloudless palette of pinks and blues, and she was folded into his arms, and his lips kept brushing her cheek. He couldn't stop kissing her, and she didn't seem to want him to stop. He was so happy—he couldn't remember ever being this happy—and he felt a deep, welling gratitude to Mrs. Dinsmoor for bringing them together again. Suddenly a man emerged from the water and began walking toward them. He moved slowly, as if he were in pain, and then Jimmy noticed that his hands were shackled at his waist.

The man was dressed in a dark business suit and tie, similar to the one Walter Plane had worn at dinner. Jimmy knew, in the way people know things in dreams, that Estella had invited Plane to join them. He was angry at her: why did she have to spoil their perfect evening together? Why did she always have to spoil everything? But as the man approached them, Jimmy saw that it was not Plane, but his Uncle Joe who was coming to summon him back home to Cortez.

Joe's shackles clanked. Jimmy's eyes blinked open. For a moment, he had no idea where he was, and then he remembered, he was in New York, the Carter Hotel. He groaned softly. He wanted to be back on the beach, holding Estella. But he was too far from sleep now, and the noise he'd heard in his dream was real—the sound of his doorknob creaking. He struggled to wakefulness as he watched the door open just wide enough for someone to slip inside. The door closed, and a room key dropped onto the covers. He pulled himself up and found himself looking at Estella, who was perched at the foot of his bed.

"Well?" she said, as if it were the most normal thing in the world for her to be sitting in his dingy hotel room, all dressed up for a night out on the town.

"What?" he said, groping for his watch.

Estella walked over to the window and pulled open the venetian blinds. Bright sunlight poured in between the slats. He squinted at her and tried to make sense of what he was seeing. The sun was shining. It must be morning. So why was she wearing that sexy little dress? Better question: Why was she here?

She picked up his sketchpad and a pencil and handed them to him. Then she moved his clothes off the chair across from the bed and settled herself there, cross-legged, facing him. "Draw me," she said.

He rubbed the sleep from his eyes and yawned. "Now?"

"You're hired. You've got the job."

He needed to pee. He needed a cup of coffee and wished she'd thought to bring him one. He was tempted to tell her to go to hell. Instead, he propped himself up against the pillows and began sketching her face. Her features were so achingly familiar to him, yet they had changed, of course, as she'd matured into a woman. The baby fat in her cheeks was gone; so, too, the pout around her mouth. Her eyes still betrayed very little of what she was feeling, but he thought he found in them a softness, a kind of vulnerability, that he hadn't seen there before.

A few minutes passed. Then she said, "This is dull. Let's make it a nude."

He watched as she removed her shoes, then slowly began to unbutton her dress. It fell to the floor and she paused, as if to give him the chance to study her in this state of half-undress. He said nothing as she unhooked her bra and slid off her panties. She stood before him, nude, a golden goddess in the morning light. "Do you want me standing or sitting?" she asked.

He wanted her any way he could have her. Swallowing hard, he said, "Either. Whatever. Both."

She remained standing. He picked up his pencil, settled the pad on his lap, and tried to catch his breath. She moved over to the window and glanced outside. Dust motes swirled over her skin as he began outlining the contours of her body—the curve of her breast, the tilt of her hip, her pulse beating so visibly at her throat. All sense of his surroundings, all sound dropped away as he focused on capturing her essence.

She had struck a pose that he knew so well: she was leaning on her right leg, and she'd stepped her left leg in front, so that her body was slanted slightly forward toward him. Rather than make her look awkward, her angled stance gave her the look of a dancer poised to begin a series of turns across the floor.

He told himself that later, when she was gone, he would allow himself to think about how beautiful she was, about how desperately he yearned to feel her naked skin against his. For now, however, he had to shut off his feelings and desires as his hand raced across the paper. He filled a page, tore it out of his pad, and began on another without a moment's break; the images were crowding so quickly into his brain that he never took his eyes off her, not even to see what he was drawing.

She seemed restless, moving from the window to the chair to the door, stepping lightly through the pile of line drawings that lay discarded on the floor. She had just settled herself on his bed when the distinctive chirping sound of a cellular telephone disturbed the silence. She shrugged her shoulders, as if to apologize for the interruption, and dug into her bag for her phone.

"Yes?" she said, then scowled. "Oh fuck! When . . . ? Where?"

He caught the expression on her face as she sat naked and chatting, as casually as if he'd seen her nude a thousand times before.

She shook her head and said, "No, you go ahead and—Right. I'll be there soon . . . I'm in midtown." She glanced at him and smiled. "With a friend." She didn't bother with a good-bye before she clicked off the phone and said, "I've got a breakfast."

He dropped the pencil and gawked at her. "Now?"

"It's morning," she said, as she hurriedly got dressed. "This is when they have them."

"But what about . . . ?" he stammered.

She had already slipped on her shoes and was at the door before he could think of a comeback. "I'll need another sitting."

"I think you'll remember." She smirked at him. And then opened the door and was gone, leaving him alone in the room. If not for the sketches scattered all over the floor, he might have thought he'd imagined her visit. He blinked his eyes, actually wondering for one crazy second whether he could make her reappear, like a genie popping out of a bottle. He glumly picked up one of the pages and stared at his work, and then suddenly he knew what he had to do.

He crumpled up the paper and leaped out of bed. He threw on his jeans and rushed out of the room so fast that he was down the stairs and in the hotel lobby before he realized that he'd forgotten his sneakers. But there was no time to waste retracing his steps, so he charged barefoot onto the busy street. He spun around on his heels, searching for Estella. When he spotted her at the corner, just getting into a taxi, he sprinted down the block, dashing through the swarms of pedestrians like an Olympic track runner, intent on the gold.

Her hand on was on the handle and she was about to close the door when he jumped in next to her.

"Hey!" the cabbie protested.

"It's okay, keep on going," Estella said.

The cabby turned on the meter and tore away from the curb.

"What are you doing?" Jimmy demanded of her.

"Well," she said pertly, "I'm going home to change for—"

He was so angry he wanted to slap her. "You know what I mean. What are you doing to me?"

She pointed to his feet. "You forgot your shoes."

All his pent-up bitterness and fury, so deeply repressed for so many years that it surprised even him, spilled out of him now. "Is this fun for you?" he snapped, fighting to keep his voice down. "Do you enjoy this? Do you enjoy hurting me? How does it feel not to feel anything?"

She flinched, and he took some comfort in seeing that he'd penetrated her usually unyielding defenses. She turned away from him, and he forced himself to stay quiet, waiting for her to respond. He watched her in profile as she stared out the window at the people streaming into the towering office buildings.

Impatient, he was about to break the silence when she turned to him and said quietly, "Let's say there was a little girl and from the moment she could understand . . . let's say she was taught to fear daylight. She was told that the day was her enemy. That it would hurt her. And then, one sunny afternoon, you ask her to go out and play, and she won't. You can't be angry with her, can you?"

The tears she refused to shed softened him.

"I was there," he said, wishing he could kiss away her suffering. "I saw the life in that girl's eyes. No matter what you say or do, I still see that."

She shook her head and turned back to the window. "What you love isn't me, what you hate isn't me. But the two together is who I am."

"I don't believe that. We're here. You and me." He grabbed her shoulder and pulled her around. "Estella, look at me," he insisted.

"I see you, Jimmy Bell," she said, as a tear she couldn't stop rolled down her cheek. "We are who we are. We don't change."

He wiped away the tear with his fingertip and whispered, "I can change."

She stared at him a moment, and her longing to believe him showed in her face—the face he knew and loved so well. But she had been too well-schooled by Mrs. Dinsmoor to put her faith in a man, especially a man who promised to love her. "Nothing changes," she said bleakly.

He took her hand. To his surprise, she allowed him to interlace their fingers. She didn't let go until the taxi pulled up in front of Mrs. Dinsmoor's brownstone on Eighty-third Street off Park Avenue.

"Well," she said, getting out of the cab. She hesitated, as if she had something on her mind she wanted to share with him. But then, with a slight shake of her head, she closed the door, and stared at him through the open window. "Thank you for the lift home. You're still a wonderful escort," she said.

He watched her as she hurried up the sidewalk and into the house, rushing to put as much distance as possible between herself and the daylight.

It was his day for visitors. He was working on one of his sketches of Estella, taking advantage of the late afternoon sun, when there was a knock at his door.

"Come in," he said, as he concentrated on applying a yellow-pink watercolor wash to Estella's thighs. When he looked up, he discovered Estella's boyfriend peering over his shoulder.

"Oh, hey . . ." He suddenly couldn't remember the man's name.

"Walter," Plane said as he took in the dozens of nude renderings of Estella scattered across Jimmy's bed.

Jimmy grinned. "Right. Hi." He stuck out his hand to shake Plane's. "So what are you doing here?"

"Estella told me she'd come over. Posed for you. I was . . ." He shrugged and picked up one of the drawings. ". . . curious, I'd guess you'd call it. Hope I'm not interrupting."

"No, it's okay." Jimmy lit a cigarette and

watched Plane examine a sketch of Estella sitting on the bed, leaning back on her elbows. Her head was raised, her throat and shoulders exposed.

"Wow," Plane said finally. "You're very good."

He sensed that Plane was being sincere. He even suspected that Plane knew what he was talking about. But the compliment, coming from the man he perceived to be his rival, meant nothing to him. He didn't believe for a second that Estella loved Plane; quite probably, she disliked him. But he was sleek and wealthy and powerful, and she'd chosen him as the vehicle she would ride on her path to self-destruction.

He understood better now than he had at seventeen the damage Mrs. Dinsmoor had inflicted on Estella. Thirty-odd years ago, a man had cruelly deserted a lonely, almost middle-aged woman who'd been tricked into thinking she was about to be blessed with a wonderful new life of marital bliss. Mrs. Dinsmoor had never recovered, and she'd hand-picked Estella to be the instrument of her revenge.

"I've got a good subject," he said.

"She's incredible." Plane shook his head and sat down on the chair. "I must be insane."

"Why?" Jimmy asked, noticing that Plane was making himself very comfortable, considering that he hadn't been invited to stay. But he was obviously the kind of guy who felt at home wherever he went.

"To risk losing her." He scooped up a stack of the sketches and flipped through them. "Jesus, look at this! And I still can't commit? That's certifiable!"

"You don't seem crazy to me."

Plane leaned forward and lowered his voice, as if he were about to divulge some very important and confidential information. "I feel like one of those cliff divers. You know, in Acapulco? I'm on the edge. The tide's right. Now's the time to leap. And I think Estella just gave me a shove."

Jimmy didn't give a damn what happened to Plane, but he didn't think he'd ever stop caring about Estella. So though he dreaded hearing the answer, he asked, "What do you mean?"

"These . . ." Plane nodded at the drawings. "You. She's trying to wake me up. I understand. I do feel bad that you were pulled into all this. She doesn't mean to hurt you. Believe me, Estella cares about you.

"That's who she is, but I do love her." He sighed, then looked at Jimmy. "You know her. You two are old friends. Can I ask your advice?"

Jimmy inhaled, blew a smoke ring, stared at Plane. For a rich guy, he was really dumb. Or maybe he was wily as a fox.

"What do you think I should do?" Plane

pressed, ignoring Jimmy's obvious reluctance to play Ann Landers. "About me and Estella? I trust your opinion."

Jimmy took one last drag, then ground his cigarette into the ashtray. "I think you two are perfect for each other."

Plane studied his face. If he was searching for signs that Jimmy was lying, he could find no evidence of it in his expression. Jimmy was telling him the truth, or at least one version of it.

"Thanks," Plane said finally. He stood up and slapped the wrinkles out of his suit. "Okay, James. I'm going to let you get back to work. Thanks for your patience. You're as talented as advertised. I look forward to your show."

"Right." Jimmy nodded. He waited until Plane closed the door. Then he picked up the pile of drawings that had made such an impression on Plane and took a long, hard look at them. He did have talent. Even he could see it in these rough sketches. It had taken the intervention of Jerry Ragno and his not-so-anonymous benefactor to revive the single-minded passion he felt when he put pencil to paper. For that alone, he owed them. There was no longer any doubt in his mind that he was going to have a show. He was determined to do whatever was necessary to make it happen.

CHAPTER 8

Ragno had left him a message at the hotel that was brief and to the point: he was to meet the lawyer on Wednesday at eight P.M. at an address in TriBeCa, a former industrial neighborhood in the throes of gentrification on the city's far lower west side. Jimmy showed up as instructed at the building, which from the outside looked like an aging warehouse. The first floor, according to a sign on the wall, was occupied by the Masala Chai Company. The thickly sweet aroma of spices and brewed tea trailed him as he rode the old-fashioned cage elevator to the fourth floor.

There was only one door on the landing, and it was open. "Hello?" Jimmy called out, wondering whether he'd written down the wrong address.

"In here," Ragno returned his greeting.

He followed Ragno's voice down a narrow hallway that led to a huge, sparsely furnished loft where he found Ragno and Erica Thrall, deep in conversation.

Ragno waved him over. "Well, what do you think?"

"Cozy," Jimmy said, impressed by the vastness of the space. He could see, through the southwest-facing windows, the skyline of downtown Manhattan as well as the lights of New Jersey twinkling across the Hudson River. He imagined the room by day, flooded with bright sunshine.

"Good," Ragno said. "It's your new home."

Jimmy glanced from him to Erica. "What are you talking about?"

Ragno pointed a bottle of Dom Perignon chilling in an ice bucket on the kitchen counter at the far end of the room. "Your opening is in ten weeks."

"If you won't be ready," Thrall said hopefully, "we'll simply reschedule for another—"

Jimmy was still absorbing Ragno's astonishing pronouncement about his new studio and living quarters. Most likely Estella had persuaded Mrs. Dinsmoor that he needed a better space and more money. "I'll be ready," he was quick to assure Thrall.

"This date is firm," she said, sounding disappointed.

Ragno said, "You'll move in here. You've got food. Paint. Canvas." He ticked off the items on his finger. "Whatever else you need, ask Erica."

If she expected him to play the humble petitioner, she was about to be disappointed. "Fine. Erica, I need money," he said, sounding as if he were only asking for exactly what he deserved. "Living expenses."

She pursed her lips disapprovingly. "I don't believe that's my—"

"Done," Ragno said. "What else?"

"Will there be publicity?"

Ragno smiled at Erica Thrall like a proud father. His expression was easy to read: *The boy catches on fast.*

Thrall's reaction was less enthusiastic. "No one's ever heard of you. It could be tricky."

He'd done his homework and learned, after consulting with Owen Tulp, that talent aside, the key to success was marketing. If he came wrapped in an interesting package, magazines such as *People* and *W* were more likely to feature him in their pages. "A commercial fisherman from the Gulf Coast winds up in the New York City art world. That's a story I'd read."

"Well, aren't we media savvy?" Thrall said,

displaying just a hint of a thaw in her chilly attitude.

He grinned at her. "We learn."

But she wasn't yet ready to make friends. She pointed to the champagne. "Toast in my absence. I'm late." Her high heels clicked against the bare wooden floor as she left him alone with Ragno.

"She hates me," Jimmy said. It occurred to him as soon as the words were out of his mouth that he didn't much care.

Ragno shrugged. "An artist dropped out. There was an opening on her—"

Jimmy cut him off. "Somebody wants to turn this frog into a prince."

"I don't understand," Ragno said.

"It looks like I've got a fairy godmother."

"I wouldn't know." Ragno picked up his briefcase and snapped shut the lock.

"Whatever you say, Spider-Man." Noticing Ragno's blank stare, he explained, "Ragno means spider in Italian."

"Right." Ragno nodded, but Jimmy could tell that the lawyer wasn't much interested in learning a new language. "I'll see you at your opening."

He waited until he heard Ragno slam the door closed before he took himself on a tour of his new home. The space consisted of one enormous room that extended the length of the building. A futon and a television set were concealed behind a tall screen at one end of the loft, and some overstuffed couches, a table, and a couple of lamps made up the living area. Besides a narrow galley kitchen, the rest of the room was meant to be his studio. He couldn't have asked for a more perfect space if he'd chosen it himself.

His inspection completed, he popped the cork on the Dom Perignon and swigged it down without bothering to look for a glass. The bottle was more than half empty when he decided to explore the rest of the building. He took the elevator to the top floor and discovered a door that led to the roof. Stepping outside, he treated himself to another healthy gulp of champagne. He was drunk, he realized, as he stumbled over to the edge of the building. He looked down and saw, spread out before him, New York with all of its promise and pain.

The city was his for the taking. Why then did he feel so hollow inside, so filled with despair? He held the bottle upside-down over the edge of the building and watched the last few drops trickle through the darkness. He wished that he hadn't opened the champagne, that he'd saved it for a real occasion. A party for one was no fun.

The ache in his chest pushed him to action. He leaned back and hurled the bottle over his head as far as he could reach. It soared through the air, arcing skyward high above him, before it tumbled end-over-end out of his sight to the pavement below. He thought, *Estella,* and then he whispered her name to the night. The only answer that came back to him was the piercing scream of an ambulance siren racing to someone else's rescue.

For the next three weeks, Jimmy left the loft only once a day for a brisk walk down Broadway to Battery Park and back. Some days he got so engrossed in work that he didn't leave the apartment at all. When he was hungry, he ordered in Chinese food or opened a can of whatever Ragno's secretary had picked up for him at the supermarket. When the phone infrequently rang, he let the machine answer it. When he ran out of paint or paper, he called Ragno, and the same harried secretary who brought the groceries delivered to his door whatever art supplies he needed.

He drew feverishly, from memory, portraits of all the people who'd meant the most to him. Often, he would wake up in the middle of the night and couldn't fall back to sleep. He would throw back the covers, pick up a brush, and paint until well past dawn, until he fell back to sleep slumped over his easel. He couldn't ever recall feeling as exhausted—or as exhilarated.

The only interruptions he allowed in his schedule were for interviews and photo sessions. Erica Thrall's publicist had gone into high gear and called all her media contacts to sell them on the most intriguing new talent to hit New York since Jean-Michel Basquiat had been discovered scribbling graffiti on walls all over downtown Manhattan: James Bell, the fisherman turned artist whose work had so excited Erica Thrall that she'd *personally* flown down to Florida to offer him a one-man show.

Jimmy was fast becoming a pro at dealing with all the photographers and stylists who arrived at the loft bearing sacks full of equipment and their own unique visions of the image they wanted him to project. He'd even reconstructed his biography to be able to seduce interviewers with a more dramatic version of his childhood—what Erica approvingly referred to as "a sexier story."

On a day so hot that it made him homesick for Cortez, the gallery owner phoned to say she was bringing over a client who might be interested in buying one or two of his portraits. She was sure, she said, he wouldn't mind if she sent over one of her assistants to help him prepare for the visit. As a special favor. Because this was all so new to him.

He did mind, and so, it seemed, did Marci, the assistant, who remembered him none too fondly from that rainy night when he'd shown up uninvited at the gallery door and dripped all over her guest list. And no matter how many times he told her the exact order in which he envisioned showing his work, she either couldn't—or didn't want to—get it right.

"No, Marci." He stood at the kitchen sink, washing brushes as he watched her screw up the sequence that made the most sense to him. He listed them for her, yet again. "Dinsmoor. Maggie. Joe, and then Estella. That order."

But dammit! She couldn't get it right. He doubted whether she could ever get it right. He dumped the rest of the brushes in the sink and stalked over to her. "Stop!" he yelled. "Stop it! Now watch." He grabbed the paintings away from her and positioned them the only way that made sense to him.

"That's what I was doing," she pouted.

"How about this?" He glared at her and stuck a dripping wet brush in her hand. "You be the overworked artist, and I'll be the dizzy assistant."

He could tell she was about to pull a major sulk when the doorbell buzzed. "Great," he muttered. Here came trouble, dressed up as Erica Thrall.

Marci rushed to the door and returned with her boss and a barrel-chested man dressed in a three-piece suit and cowboy boots.

"James Bell, meet Ted Fabinowitz, a dear friend and major collector," Thrall said. "From Fort Worth, Texas, of all places."

"A pleasure," Fabinowitz drawled.

Jimmy gave the Texan a perfunctory handshake, then went back to washing his brushes.

"Teddy, James' paintings are along the wall over there," Thrall said. She shot Jimmy a disapproving look behind her client's back, not very different from the one Maggie would use to communicate to him: *Behave yourself—or else!* "Take your time. I'll be right here," she told Fabinowitz.

She dispatched Marci to answer whatever questions Fabinowitz might have, then thrust a copy of *W* magazine at Jimmy. "Page thirty-seven. Delicious. See how it's all coming together? Just as I promised, James Bell frenzy. Perception is everything. Imagine what'll happen when they actually see your wonderful work?"

Erica produced another copy of the article and tacked it to the bulletin board that hung in the kitchen. Pinned to the board were brief mentions, articles, and pictures of Jimmy that had previously appeared in the tabloid gossip columns, the *Village Voice,* and other local press.

Jimmy grunted a noncommittal response as he scanned the article entitled, "Fishing for Success: The Hands of the Artist James Bell." A black-and-white photograph of his hands appeared on the opposite page. He didn't bother reminding Erica that launching a publicity blitz had been his idea, not hers. He didn't need the credit, so long as he got results.

Erica reached into her bag and pulled out two envelopes. "Your beloved per diem, and an invitation to the Hamilton Museum Benefit."

He stuck the per diem check in his pocket and ignored the second envelope. "Toss it," he said. Benefits were bullshit. He didn't have time to kiss up to rich assholes like Plane.

"I killed a publicist for it," Erica said, shoving the engraved invitation into his hand. "This is *the* event, darling. Black tie. Big money. New money, old money. *Everybody* will be there."

Division of labor: His job was to provide the paintings. It was up to her to show up at events and make the connections. He was about to tell her what she could do with her black tie and big money when the phone rang. As he went to answer it, he could hear Erica gushing to Fabinowitz, "Ted, you see why I was so excited. This is a fresh . . . well, it's a new portrait vocabulary, isn't it?"

He grabbed the receiver and said, "Hello?"

"Jimmy?"

It took him a couple of seconds to recover from the shock of hearing her voice. "Estella," he said.

He'd dreamed of her repeatedly over the last month, the same dream of them dancing in each other's arms on the beach. But something had changed in him since the day he'd chased after her in his bare feet. He'd come to New York in pursuit of her, not of his art. Now that he was painting again, he'd moved past being the lovesick boy who would sacrifice his life to save the sad little girl in the dark tower.

Someone—who else could it be but Mrs. Dinsmoor?—had granted him one chance to make his mark. He had no more time to waste dancing with Estella, except in his dreams. He was too busy rediscovering himself as an artist. His every demand was being met. Great things were expected of him. It said so in all the articles on the bulletin board. And if you couldn't believe your press clippings, what could you believe?

"I was wondering . . ." Her voice faltered, and she stumbled a bit over the words. "I'm sure that you're busy with everything. But maybe we could get together? I'd like to see you if—"

He looked across the room and watched Erica pitching him to Fabinowitz. "This is really a bad time. My show's coming up. Maybe after."

"Please," she said, so softly he almost doubted he'd heard her correctly.

There was something she needed from him badly enough that she was prepared to beg for it. He would have to see her, if only because he was curious to know what she wanted.

She wanted to take him to lunch at the Boathouse Cafe in Central Park, but he said he was too busy, so they settled instead for a walk in the park. He slotted her in between appointments: a photography session for which Erica had sent over a stylishly tailored suit for him to wear, and an interview with a reporter from *ArtForum* magazine. Estella suggested they meet at the Bow Bridge. When she started to give him directions, he cut her off because Erica was signalling him to hang up so he could talk to Fabinowitz.

He told her not to worry, he'd find her. But when he reached the Boathouse, on the eastern end of the lake near Seventy-second Street, he couldn't even see the bridge, much less figure out how to get there. "Just follow the path past the angel," a teenager on rollerblades said vaguely.

It took him five minutes to find the angel, an imposing stone statue that stood guard over a paved plaza, and another five minutes to figure out where to go from there. He hurried along a dirt path in what he hoped was the right direction, until he spotted a small, gently curved bridge that spanned a narrow neck of the lake. Estella was leaning on her elbows, staring down at the water. The girl he'd known in his childhood would have chastised him for keeping her waiting, but the woman she'd grown into seemed too absorbed in her thoughts even to notice he was late.

"Don't jump," he called as he approached her.

She turned and smiled at him. "Would you save me?"

"Not in this suit," he said, coming up to join her.

She stood back and took a long look at him. "Very handsome. Looks like your dreams are coming true."

"Thrall's happy," he said, more pleased by her compliment than he cared to admit to himself. "She says the show will get good reviews. I don't want to jinx it."

He'd thought he was over her. Why then was it almost too painful to stand by her side? He ran his hands over the painted stone surface of the bridge and tried to distract himself with the scenery. A weeping willow drooped gracefully over the edge of the lake, where a family of ducks swam in circles searching for food. An elderly couple, enjoying the warm sun on this balmy late summer afternoon, held hands as they strolled along the path that bordered the water. On the other side of the lake, a group of high school students were playing Frisbee on the lawn. The atmosphere was so peaceful and bucolic that except for the elegant buildings that rose above the park to the east and west, he might have thought he'd been transported to a tranquil country meadow where people had come for the day to picnic.

When the silence between them felt too thick, he asked, "What about you? I guess you're not much of a dreamer?"

She smiled again and started walking toward the west side. "I have some," she said.

"Name one," he challenged her.

She looked at him, and he knew what she was thinking: *Can I trust you with my dreams?* "I'd like to restore my aunt's house," she said at last, leading him up a narrow dirt path edged with trees and shrubbery so thick that he couldn't see beyond them.

It was the last thing he'd expected her to say. "Why?" he asked, and reached for her hand as she stumbled on a tree root that stuck out of the ground.

"It's incredible. A little spooky. Definitely neglected. But that's on the outside. It's just . . . lonely. All it needs is some life. Someone to care, you know, to love it again. It would come back. It would be beautiful."

As she spoke, he was back there again, seeing Paradiso Perduto for the very first time. She was absolutely right. The mansion *was* lonely and neglected. And yet, he had a sense that she was talking about so much more than just the mansion. She had dropped his hand now that they were on more level ground, but he could still feel the imprint of her fingers, warm and moist, on his.

"Does she ever ask about me?" he asked. "Your aunt?"

"She doesn't have to. She knows everything you're doing."

"How?" he asked, although he was pretty sure he knew the answer. Through Ragno, of course. The lawyer no doubt had to send her weekly progress reports.

She shrugged. He wondered, as they started climbing down a slight incline, when she'd last been home. They reached the bottom of the hill and had to choose between two roadways that lay in front of them. She was walking slightly ahead of him, and she made the decision. She turned left and led them into a wide tunnel that came out onto one of the main roadways.

They'd almost reached the other end of the tunnel when she said, "Walter wants to marry me."

She'd stopped walking so abruptly that he almost bumped into her. Her words echoed through the tunnel: *Marry me. Marry me.*

And still he wasn't sure he'd heard her correctly. He shook his head, and she repeated herself. "He's asked me to marry him."

"Really." He made it a statement, not a question. He wasn't at all surprised. In fact, she seemed more stunned by Plane's proposal than he was.

"Well, not asked. More like begged. It was kind of embarrassing for—"

"Why are you telling me this?" he asked.

"Because . . . because we're . . ." She shook her head, as if she were more puzzled by her revelation than he was. "I thought you'd want to—"

"Right," he said briskly. He cast about for the proper thing to say. "Well, congratulations. I hope . . . I'm sure you'll be very happy."

She was staring at him through the dimness. Once again, he had the impression that she was pleading with him, but he didn't know what she wanted, and he was tired of playing guessing games with her. Suddenly, he felt a great need to put distance between himself and Estella Dinsmoor. He gave her a perfunctory kiss on the cheek and said, "I gotta meet somebody. An editor at *ArtForum*. Business."

He started walking briskly toward the light at the far end of the tunnel. "Wait," she said, and when he turned around to face her, her eyes searched his for understanding. "Listen, I know Walter's an acquired taste. But he does love me."

She hadn't said whether she loved Walter. It didn't matter. She wasn't going to have a change of heart. And he wasn't going to speak the feelings that were locked in his.

"I'm late," he said, forcing a smile. He turned his back on her so that she couldn't see the pain that must be showing in his face.

"Good luck," she called to him.

He raised his hand in acknowledgment and forced himself to keep walking until he came out the other side of the tunnel. A ball rolled to a stop at his feet. A few yards away, a young man and a little boy waved their arms, motioning for him to return the ball. As he bent to pick it up, he heard the distant rumble of thunder. To the west, he could see a thin line of dark clouds marching toward the city. He tossed the ball back and started running. A storm was predicted, and he wanted to get home before it hit. Some situations could be avoided. There were others from which he would never learn how to protect himself.

"I was an orphan," Jimmy said into the tape recorder.

Ruth Shepard, the pretty, thirtyish writer whom *ArtForum* had sent to interview him, nodded encouragingly.

"My Uncle Joe raised me," he said, pointing to his portrait of Joe. "He was a dope smuggler."

Raindrops thrummed a staccato tattoo against his windows. The evening sky looked dark and ominous, but the loft was brightly lit and cheerful. Jimmy smiled bravely for Ruth Shepard. She seemed like a nice person, warm and friendly. At his suggestion, she'd removed her wet shoes, and her stockinged feet made little catlike thumping sounds as she followed him around the room.

"Joe spent most of the seventies in Rainford Penitentiary. When I was thirteen, I found Joe dead in our living room. He'd OD'ed." He averted his eyes, to impress upon her that the memory of his grief was still fresh.

The first few times he'd told the story, which belonged to his next-door neighbor, he'd stumbled over some of the details. By now, he'd repeated it so often that he'd made it his own. "I . . . I lost the apartment, lived in an abandoned car for a couple of years."

"My God," she exclaimed, stroking his arm sympathetically.

He thought he saw tears welling in her dark, liquid brown eyes, so he hastened to assure her, "It wasn't so bad. It was a big car. A 'sixty-eight Riviera."

When he was a kid, the Riviera was his dream car, turquoise-blue with soaring fins and a huge, wide body. He'd kept a picture of it for years, fantasizing that some day he would buy himself one.

He put his hand in the small of Ruth's back and led her over to Mrs. Dinsmoor's portrait. He felt her leaning slightly into his hand. She was small and dark, and looked nothing like Estella, which was perhaps what he liked best about her.

The phone shrilled. "The machine will get it," he said, wanting to preserve the mood.

"So after your uncle died?" she prompted him.

"I wound up crewing on a Panamanian freighter until I came here."

His outgoing message reeled to its end, and Erica Thrall's voice rang out across the room. "Good, you're gone. I hope this means you're in your tux, charming high society at the Hamilton bash. Remember, smile, darling, and call me in the morning."

"Erica." He rolled his eyes at Ruth.

"You *are* smiling," she said as she padded past the picture of Mrs. Dinsmoor. She stopped in front of Estella's portrait. "Wonderful eyes. Who is she?"

"A girl from Florida," he said offhandedly. He was on the verge of launching into his story about the Florida girl: he'd loved her when they were kids only to realize (alas!) when he'd remet her as an adult that she was really rather superficial, not at all his type.

But before he could get started, the cassette in Ruth's tape machine clicked off. "One sec," she said and extracted the full tape. She dug in her bag and found a blank cassette, which she dropped on the floor as she tried to insert it into the machine.

Jimmy bent to retrieve the cassette. Their palms brushed as she took it from him, and her hand seemed to linger in his longer than was absolutely necessary. He couldn't help but think how nice it would feel to have company in his bed.

"Those scars," she said, staring at his hand.

He rested his hand, palm up, in hers.

"Tiger shark," he said.

Her eyes widened as she ran her thumb across the two-inch scar, a souvenir of the time he'd grabbed too quickly for a gutting knife. Her caress was the next best thing to a promise. There was a bottle of wine in the refrigerator. He was about to suggest that they have a drink when he looked up and saw, over Ruth's shoulder, his portrait of Estella.

"Does it still hurt?" Ruth asked.

"Yes," he whispered, staring at Estella.

She followed his eyes to the picture. "Something wrong?"

Everything was wrong, but maybe there was something he could do to fix it. A man couldn't be faulted for holding onto hope. "What time is it?" he asked.

"Almost seven. Why?"

The Hamilton gala had started with cocktails at six-thirty. Finding a cab would be impossible because of the rain, and he still had to change his clothes. Erica was going to kill him.

"I have to go," he told Ruth.

He'd given her plenty of material. The interview was officially ended.

* * *

He'd never before worn a tuxedo. As he climbed the stairs to the Hamilton Museum, he tugged at the cummerbund around his waist. He thought of all the Cary Grant and Fred Astaire movies he'd seen as a kid. They'd always seemed so relaxed and comfortable in their evening clothes. He felt trussed up like a roasting chicken. And there stood Erica, at the top of the steps, looking as if she were ready to throw him on the spit and broil him.

"Well, you're fashionably rude," she snapped as soon as he was within hearing distance. "Listen, I've got hordes of people you simply must meet."

He whisked past her and hurried into the main entrance room of the museum, ignoring her indignant demands that he wait for her.

The Hamilton was housed in a Beaux Art–style mansion that had formerly belonged to one of New York's richest founding families. The mansion, and many of the museum's most important pieces, had been donated by the Hamiltons, and several family members were still actively involved on the board. The guests at this evening's benefit were a heterogeneous mix of aging aristocrats and the newly arrived power elite. The common denominator among them was money and power. White-haired dowagers mingled with real-estate moguls; Wall Street tycoons sipped champagne with supermodels who were hardly out of their teens.

The room reeked of status and glamour. As Jimmy moved through the crowd, people called to him, greeted him by name, offered their congratulations. But he felt like an intruder, there under false pretenses. He was already famous, it seemed, and they hadn't even seen his work yet. They were so eager to embrace him, and all because the publicity machine had anointed him the crown prince of glitz.

On any other night, he would have obeyed Erica's orders and dutifully worked the room. Tonight, however, he was on a mission. He was searching for Estella.

When he spotted Walter Plane, he knew he'd come to the right place. Estella couldn't be far away. Plane, who was accompanied by Owen Tulp and Lois Marx, as well as a large black man whom Jimmy didn't recognize, beckoned to him to join them.

Jimmy nodded hello and headed in the opposite direction. He couldn't trust himself right now not to haul off and punch Plane in the nose.

"James, wait a minute," Plane called. He pushed his way over to Jimmy and said, "I wanted to call. To congratulate you on your success. Jesus, you're all over the place. The man of the hour. We're both very proud of you."

It was the "both" that bothered him most. Plane had a lot of nerve, speaking for Estella. "Excuse me," he said, not even trying to sound polite. But before he could make his escape, he was ambushed by Plane's sidekicks.

"James, I'm so glad I ran into you," said Owen, pumping his hand. "My dear friend's decorating his first house. House?" he hooted. "*Pulleeze!* This is a castle. Anyhow, he desperately needs art—"

Lois leaned in to air-kiss him on both cheeks. "Ask about his commission," she sniped.

"Bitch!" Owen shot back.

"We just got the Thrall invite. So exciting," Lois raved.

"The boy with the hands! I saw your spread. Anton La Farge," the black man introduced himself.

"Be nice to Anton, James," Plane said. "He's got a lot of empty walls."

"I'm taking my time," Anton told Jimmy.

"You're counting your money. Don't worry, James is still reasonable." Plane turned to Jimmy. "I forget, how did you charge? Was it canvas size? Per gallon of paint?"

He smiled expansively as his little band of hangers-on awarded him with a wave of appreciative laughter. On a roll now, he said, "Maybe it's volume. You know, by the lot size. Like T-shirts. Just churn the stuff out."

Jimmy promised himself the opportunity to show Plane how shark fishermen from Cortez evened their scores. That demonstration could wait, however. His sole purpose for being here this evening was to find Estella. Nothing, not even Plane's pathetic attempts to be humorous at his expense, would deter him.

"Come on, James, remind me," Plane hounded him. "How do you decide its worth?"

"By its beauty," Estella replied, coming up behind Jimmy. "Does it move you? Do you want it? Can you live without it?"

"There you are." Plane smiled and reached for her hand.

Jimmy turned to her. "I have to talk to you," he said urgently.

"Another time," Plane said. "We're late."

"We just got here," Estella protested.

Plane shook his head. "Dinner. The Barrows are waiting at Perfume." He put his arm around her shoulders and gave Jimmy a friendly pat on the back. "Say good-bye," he told Estella.

She said nothing but allowed Plane to lead her out of the room. Just as she reached the doorway, she glanced at Jimmy over her shoulder.

"Lovely couple," Anton said.

Erica, steering a white-haired man by the elbow, bore down upon Jimmy. "Senator, this is the young artist I've been telling you about," she said to her companion.

Jimmy drifted away before she had a chance to finish the introductions. Lost in a fantasy about rescuing Estella from Plane's evil clutches, he walked through the press of guests, toward the door.

Owen suddenly appeared in front of him. "So can I put you together with my decorator friend, Burton?" he demanded.

"Excuse me," Jimmy said, trying to move past him.

But Owen had his own fantasy, and he was not to be so easily deterred. "I think Erica's the best. But you have no idea who I know in this city, James. I could make you—"

"I'm sorry," Jimmy said.

"It's all about relationships," Owen said. He grabbed Jimmy's arm, but Jimmy yanked himself free. As he tried to shove Owen out of his way, Owen lost his balance and slid feet first onto the marble floor. That made twice he'd accidentally brought the man to his knees.

But he couldn't afford to stick around to apologize. He briskly exited the building, just in time to see Plane guiding Estella into a black stretch limousine that had been waiting for them in front of the museum. He watched the limo pull away from the curb. Rain was pelting down on him, but he couldn't be bothered to go back for his umbrella. He couldn't let Estella go, not without a fight.

She wanted to be saved from Plane. He had seen the plea in her eyes when she'd glanced at him over her shoulder. For all her tough talk, she didn't know how to protect herself, so he would have to do it for her. The shield she hid behind was not so thick as to be impenetrable.

Mrs. Dinsmoor had concealed herself within the crumbling walls of the mansion, but she'd made her life a living death. That was her choice, her own doing. Estella deserved better. She'd entered Mrs. Dinsmoor's home as an innocent little girl. Day after day, year after year, she'd been forced to contemplate a horrifying mask of twisted emotions. Mrs. Dinsmoor's distorted vision had been so all-pervasive that Estella had adopted it as her own.

She had been raised in a universe of opposites. She'd mastered Mrs. Dinsmoor's distorted sense of logic: black was white, love was hate, bad was good. And when she was old enough and sufficiently schooled, Mrs. Dinsmoor had sent her out into the world armed with one simple conviction: *Men must pay.*

But Mrs. Dinsmoor had failed to understand that her plot to wreak vengeance was doomed to failure. In winning Plane's heart, Estella had only succeeded in sealing her own fate as a victim. Jimmy couldn't permit such a thing to happen. If he achieved nothing else in life, he wanted at least to know that he'd done everything in his power to rescue her.

Because of the rain, traffic was snarled on Madison Avenue. The limo slowly eased into the halting flow of cars that were stalled at the red light. Jimmy jogged toward it, hoping to catch up before the light changed. But he was too late. The limo made the light, turned left onto Fifth Avenue, and picked up speed.

He threw up his arm to hail a cab, but there were none available. He started running, keeping a close watch on the limo in case the driver signalled a turn. His legs churning, his arms gyrating like windmills in a squall, he sprinted along the sidewalk as the limo slowly moved southward. Owen had said they were going to Perfume. Jimmy guessed it was a restaurant, but he had no idea where it was. For all he knew, it could be way downtown in SoHo, or maybe even in his own neighborhood of TriBeCa.

He chased the car for blocks, past Trump Tower and St. Patrick's Cathedral, past the main branch of the New York Public Library, past the Empire State Building. He was only vaguely conscious of how far he'd run, even less aware of his surroundings. He was oblivious to the relentless rain and the blister erupting on his right heel. His entire being was solely focused on keeping the limo well within his sight.

Somewhere below Twenty-first Street, the car turned left, then continued on a couple more minutes until it pulled up in front of a nondescript building. The word PERFUME was stencilled in yellow above the fatigue-green canopy that guarded the cinder-block entrance to the restaurant. A row of limos lined the block on both sides of the street. As Jimmy struggled to catch his breath, he watched the limo driver hold an umbrella over Estella and Plane so that they wouldn't get wet as they hurried into the restaurant.

He gave them a minute to get seated, and himself enough time to stop gasping for breath. Then he followed them inside. He located them easily at a booth in the middle of the small, intimate dining room that was decorated with an Asian motif. The young woman at the reservation desk tried to stop him, but he whisked past her and swiftly crossed the room.

Estella and Plane were seated with another couple. They were to have dinner with the Barrows, Plane had said. Estella was the first to look up as Jimmy approached the booth. Her eyes widened, and she shook her head slightly, as if to warn him away.

"Is it raining?" Plane said. He smiled and pointed to the damp spot where water from

Jimmy's tuxedo had dripped onto the table. "I'd offer you a—"

He may as well have been talking to himself for all the attention Jimmy paid him.

"May I have the pleasure of this dance?" he asked Estella.

The Barrows exchanged nervous glances with each other. Plane looked from Jimmy to Estella, but Estella ignored him. "Do you know how?" she said, staring at Jimmy as if she could never tear her eyes away from him.

He smiled broadly. "Oh yeah, I can dance."

She stood up and said, without so much as a glance in Plane's direction, "Excuse me."

Music was playing softly in the background as he led her into the middle of the floor. The room was small, not meant for dancing. But when she gave him her hand, he was back again in the ballroom at Paradiso Perduto, where he'd learned to be her partner. He smiled at her. She returned the smile. Over her shoulder, he could see Plane watching them.

Estella leaned her head on his shoulder and sighed. Her breath was like a gentle breeze on his cheek. She whispered, "You smell like—"

He pulled back slightly and smiled.

"The ocean," she said, and she smiled, too. Her eyes told him she was thinking of the same moment he was—his very first visit to Paradiso Perduto.

They spun around the floor, swaying and dipping and twirling as they had done for so many hours under Mrs. Dinsmoor's critical gaze. A decade had passed since he'd held her in his arms and danced with her to the gentle rhythms of a love song. But the years seemed to have vanished. They were seventeen again, and they still owned their childhood dreams and fantasies.

When she leaned in to him, her limbs felt melded to his. They were moving in perfect unison, as if they'd spent days rehearsing for this moment. Though the entire room was watching them, they had no awareness of their audience. Their performance was for themselves alone, and it was the best they'd ever given.

He spun her around one final time as the song ended. She curtseyed to him, and he answered her with a bow. The onlookers clapped in appreciation. Even Plane attempted a smile.

Jimmy held his hand out to Estella, and they walked toward the door. The rain had let up only slightly, and neither of them had thought to grab an umbrella before they made their exit. But Estella didn't seem to mind getting soaked. She threw back her head, stuck out her tongue to taste the rain, and began to giggle. Her laughter was so contagious that Jimmy began to laugh, too. She looked so beautiful and happy that he had to touch her. He brushed the wet hair away from her forehead and kissed her eyelids. She stopped laughing and suddenly got very serious. He moved closer and kissed her hungrily on the lips.

When she kissed him back, hard on the mouth, he knew that whatever else might happen, tonight they would be together. They would make love, and he would try to tell her, without words, all the things he wanted to share with her. Afterward, she would have to make a choice—whether to join him in the daylight, or to remain in the shadows with Walter Plane.

He woke up the next morning to leaden skies, heavy rain beating against the loft windows, and the sight of Estella next to him in bed. She was smiling as he turned to look at her.

"What?" he said, reaching for her hand.

She stroked his cheek and traced a finger across his lips. "I know this face," she whispered.

He kissed her palm and held it to his cheek, wishing he could make this moment last forever. But she was already pushing aside the covers and slipping out of bed before he could stop her.

The longing welled up in him as he watched her walk naked across the room and curl up like a small child in a chair next to the window.

"Jimmy," she said, and then she sighed. "I

have to go away for a week or so. Home. I owe my aunt a visit.''

Alarmed to hear her speak of leaving, he said, ''You'll be back—''

''For your show?'' she anticipated his question. ''Yes, of course.''

She lit a cigarette, took a drag, and exhaled a cloud of smoke against the cold window pane. Almost as if she were talking to herself, she said, ''I do love the way you dance.''

Last night had been the fulfillment of his waking fantasies, the pleasure so sweet that he'd fought sleep rather than waste a second of it. He'd finally drifted off at daybreak, his arms wrapped tightly about her, daring to dream that she would draw on his strength and decide to stay with him. Now, however, watching her in the gloomy gray light from the storm, he saw that she seemed bathed in melancholy. He could take from her expression no assurances that she would make the right choice. He could only hope that these few hours they'd spent together had persuaded her of what he knew to be the truth: They loved each other. What could be more important than that?

CHAPTER 9

In the last frenzied month before his show, Jimmy turned down all requests for interviews, ignored the frequent ringing of the telephone, and rarely bothered to listen to the messages that accumulated on his answering machine. He didn't leave the loft. He hardly ate. He slept almost not at all. Summer turned into fall, the heat faded into the crisp bite of autumn, the trees in Central Park turned glorious shades of orange and gold, purple and red. He missed the entire change of season. His reality had come to be defined by canvas and paint, and the memories he drew upon to feed his creativity.

He dug deep into his childhood and found shards of discarded recollections: his mother hanging out the laundry on a windy day; his father washing the same car in which he'd died; a fisherman who'd just been told his boat had capsized in a storm: a drunken red-faced sailor who'd tried to pick a fight with Joe; the Rhinebolds' mother, her face crumpled in pain after hearing that her husband had been badly hurt in a bar brawl; a fat, sweaty man pulling up his suspenders as he left Maggie's bedroom.

Erica had criticized his work for being too safe, and he was indebted to her for that, if for nothing else. He'd pushed himself to take more risks with his painting, approaching each blank canvas with a sense of freedom and infinite possibility. He'd adopted a looser, edgier idiom. The results were unpredictable and astonishing, even to him.

Splat! A glob of red paint found its way onto his mother's cheek. *Thwat!* The fat man had suddenly grown another leg. The rage he felt toward Walter Plane showed on the face of the drunken sailor. His torment over Estella was reflected in Louise Rhinebold's expression. His portraits were informed by the whole spectrum of his emotions. He understood now what Erica and Owen had meant by dangerous. Danger extended well beyond the realm of the physical. What could be more menacing than the gleam in Walter Plane's eye as he'd watched Jimmy dancing with Estella?

Erica had said she wanted fifteen new portraits for his show. Motivated by reasons he couldn't—or chose not to—comprehend, he drove himself to the limits of his artistic energy and accomplished in ten weeks what should have taken six months. He worked almost up until the minute that Erica's movers arrived to transport his canvases to the gallery and was able to send her two more than she'd specified.

There was only enough time to take a quick shower, change his clothes, and gulp down a beer before the limo arrived to whisk him away to the opening night party. Riding uptown in the back of the limo, drinking the champagne that Erica had so thoughtfully provided, he felt far less excited about being the star of the evening than he did about seeing Estella. He'd thought of her often in his near-delirium state of the last several weeks. Sometimes, he'd heard her whispering in his ear, *That's good, Jimmy. I like that.* But he hadn't seen her, nor had they spoken. After tonight, however, everything would be different between them.

He allowed himself a minute to smoke a cigarette as he stood outside the gallery and peered through the windows at the people gathered to celebrate his good fortune. All but a handful were total strangers—wealthy friends of Erica's, prospective buyers, art enthusiasts, and critics. They would all smile and wish him well, but he knew that as soon as he turned his back, they'd be sniping about his technique, slamming his choice of colors, decrying his success. He didn't give a damn, so long as they bought his paintings and touted him to their friends as the next David Salle, the best they'd seen since Julian Schnabel.

How things had changed since the night he'd arrived in New York and been turned away from the gallery. He took a deep breath and approached the entrance. A knot of people, recognizing his face, parted down the middle to create a path for him as if he were royalty. And here came Marci, her list of invitees in hand, to personally usher him inside.

She kissed his cheek and said, "It's a great party. Congratulations."

"Thanks," he said distractedly. "Have you seen Estella? Is she here yet?"

She checked her list and shook her head. "Not yet. I'll send her to you."

"So, James." Ragno slipped up behind him. "All your dreams come true?"

He nodded automatically, though the question had barely registered, and walked into the gallery. The first person he saw was Erica, standing in front of his portrait of Maggie. She threw him a kiss across the room and raised her champagne glass in tribute to what he'd accomplished. She was talking to Anton La Farge, whom he'd met at the Hamilton Museum. Anton . . . the one who had all the empty walls. Anton was nodding as he sipped his champagne. Had he already picked out the portrait he wanted to hang in his home?

Jimmy moved through the crowd, smiling,

shaking hands, basking in the unaccustomed delight of being the guest of honor. He spotted Lois Marx deep in conversation with the Barrows. As he slipped by, he heard her describing him as a long-time friend as she praised his painting of the drunken sailor.

James Bell. . . . His name was on everyone's lips. Even those who couldn't claim to know him personally—which included almost everybody in the room—were talking about his family and his childhood as if they'd watched him growing up themselves. New Yorkers worshipped the media, and he was the media darling of the moment. A week from now, he would probably be old news. Tonight, he was enjoying his fifteen minutes of fame, which Andy Warhol had promised to anyone who bothered to grab for the brass ring.

A short, dark-haired woman tapped him on the shoulder. It took him a second to place her. Ruth Shepard, from *ArtForum.* The woman he'd almost slept with. She hugged him and whispered in his ear, "Give me a call."

He nodded obligingly and almost fell over Erica, who had walked up behind him. "You're my personal deity," she declared and handed him a glass of champagne.

Cynically wondering how often she switched religions, he asked the question that most concerned him: "Have you seen Estella?"

Erica shook her head and frowned. "Uh-oh. You've got other things to worry about."

He glanced over his shoulder and saw Owen bringing over a stooped, sour-faced man. "Carter MacLeish," Erica hissed. "The art critic for *The New York Times*."

As he turned around to greet MacLeish, he gaped unbelievingly at the familiar face he saw pressed against the outside of the window. His Uncle Joe was staring at the party scene from the other side of the glass. Uncle Joe, here in New York! Jimmy had sent him and Maggie an invitation, but in a million years he wouldn't have expected either one of them actually to show up. He should have known better. Because here was Joe in a rented tux that looked to be a couple of sizes too large, so that his uncle bore a more than passing resemblance to a circus clown who'd forgotten to put on his makeup.

Jimmy sighed. "Perfect," he muttered to himself.

He could easily imagine the argument his aunt and uncle would have had when Joe had announced that he was coming to New York. Maggie must have been furious at him for "throwing away good money," as she would have put it, to show up where he didn't belong. But Joe had obviously persisted in his quiet way. Perhaps he'd even tried to coax her into joining him. But Maggie, for all her fascination with the rich and famous, would have been too nervous about wearing the wrong clothes, saying the wrong thing. She would have nagged Joe, trying to wear him down, telling him over and over again, "We won't fit in with his fancy new friends."

He wished Joe had listened to her. For once, she would have been right.

"The man of the hour." Erica introduced him to the *Times* critic as MacLeish and Owen came over to join them. "James, meet Carter MacLeish of the *Times.*"

The two men shook hands. Erica said, "You know Ruth."

"Yep," Jimmy said. "Old friends."

It was hard to concentrate on the discussion flowing around him when his attention was so totally focused on Joe's attempts to get past Marci at the door. She was playing her usual guard dog routine, and Jimmy could only pray that Joe wouldn't succeed in wearing her down.

Sharp pangs of guilt stabbed at him. Uncle Joe, the only person in the world who loved him without any doubts or reservations. Who'd taken him into his home and heart. Who'd protected him for so many years from Maggie's harsh words and even harsher slaps. Who'd wiped away his tears and cheered his every accomplishment. Jimmy hadn't spoken to him or Maggie in weeks . . . or was it months? He'd bought them a postcard at the Empire State Building, but now, come to think of it, he wasn't sure he'd ever mailed it. He'd been so damn busy. He'd figured Joe would understand.

So why didn't his uncle understand that he had no business being here tonight? All he'd have to do was open his mouth, and he'd reveal the fact that he was an uneducated slob from a backwater fishing village who didn't have a lick of culture or sophistication. It wasn't that Jimmy was ashamed of him. Joe was a great guy. But he should have stayed home in Cortez, instead of coming here where he would only make a fool of himself and Jimmy, too, in the process.

He turned his back so that Joe couldn't catch his eye and smiled at MacLeish, who was addressing him.

"Well, you won't be painting my portrait," the critic was saying.

"No?" Jimmy glanced sideways at Erica, trying to gauge her reaction to MacLeish's comment. The *Times* carried enormous influence among gallery-goers and prospective buyers. A negative review by the paper's most respected art critic could virtually shatter his growing reputation. Was MacLeish's remark an indication that he hated Jimmy's work?

"You couldn't afford him," Erica said lightly.

MacLeish chuckled. "I'm ruined-looking enough without you."

Erica and Owen laughed along with him, and Jimmy managed a weak smile of relief. A joke from Carter MacLeish was a good sign. The relief turned to panic, however, when he heard a voice only inches away from him cry out, "Chub-chub!"

Suddenly, there was Uncle Joe, beaming as he shouted out Jimmy's childhood nickname and held out his arms for a hug. "I'm sorry," Marci said, coming up behind Joe. "I tried to—"

"It's okay," Jimmy said miserably.

Uncle Joe seemed to sense that Jimmy wasn't in a hugging mood, so he awkwardly dropped one arm, and extended the other to shake his hand instead. "Jimmy. How about this?" he whooped.

Jimmy wished Joe would lower his voice. They weren't out in the middle of the ocean, for Chrissake. People were staring at them. Joe was making a spectacle of himself.

"Hey," he said, as enthusiastically as he could manage. "What are you doing here?"

Joe's windburned face glowed with pride. "Where else would I be? Look at you, Jimmy!"

"Yeah," Jimmy said. He was acutely aware of Erica and the others gathered around him, waiting to learn the identity of this strange character with the funny accent and the ill-fitting tuxedo. Was it just his imagination, or was Joe actually giving off the not-so-faint odor of fish?

"I . . . I had to change, you know, in a car," Joe said nervously, beginning to react to Jimmy's lukewarm welcome. "This tux . . . Diane said, 'Rent a tux,' so I—"

Jimmy nodded. Diane . . . That must be one of the Rhinebold twins. How had she become involved with Joe's wardrobe choices? He couldn't cope with his friends hearing a description of Joe's shopping expedition, so before Joe could get into the details, he said, "Looks great."

Joe turned to the group and stuck his hand out to any taker. "Joe Coleman," he introduced himself. "Jimmy's uncle."

"From Florida?" MacLeish asked.

The realization of impending disaster hit Jimmy at the precise moment that Joe smiled and said, "That's right." All those lies he'd told to interviewers that they'd so obligingly printed in their articles . . . All his stories about his childhood and Joe's alleged criminal past . . .

"Uncle Joe? The drug smuggler?" Ruth Shepard shook her head in confusion. "I thought you were dead."

"Drugs?" Joe said. "No, I've been sober—"

"No." Jimmy jumped in to try and salvage his reputation. As he struggled to come up with a plausible explanation, he stammered, "See, that's—"

Erica seemed to have intuited that they were treading on dangerous ground. In an attempt to change the subject, she said, "James, Carter can't believe this is your first show."

"It's not," Joe bragged, eager to set the record straight. "Jimmy had a big art show at Washington Federal a few—"

Jimmy groaned inwardly and said, "It wasn't—"

"Washington Federal? I don't know that gallery," MacLeish said, sounding dismayed by the notion of a gallery whose existence he'd overlooked.

"Well, it's a bank," Joe explained. "Savings and loan."

"Yes, but this is my first gallery show," Jimmy said, seized by the urge to bolt out the door and run as far away from these people as his legs could carry him. He didn't dare glance at Erica or Ruth, for fear of what he might read in their expressions now that he'd been exposed as a liar and a fake.

Only Carter MacLeish seemed unconscious of the drama unfolding in front of him. "You're self-taught?" he asked.

"It was a gift. Jimmy had it," Joe proudly answered for his nephew. "Two months old, his aunt and I took him to the beach, he sat there and drew in the sand.''

''I don't remember that,'' Jimmy said. He made a mental note to tell the story the next time he was interviewed. It was so good he would have hought that Joe had made it up, except that Joe was incapable of lying, especially about something as important to him as Jimmy's childhood.

Encouraged by the apparent interest of his listeners, Joe warmed to his subject and recalled one of his favorite memories. ''One night, when was it, third grade? He took all of Maggie's best perfume and drew with it out on the street. Just poured it all out and lit it! Damn thing, whoosh! On fire, all those pretty designs. Just . . . whoosh!''

He grinned as he threw back his burly arms to describe an arc like the one that had erupted that evening in front of their apartment building. He couldn't have known that a waiter carrying a tray of champagne glasses would choose just that moment to pass by. His right arm slammed into the waiter's chest, the tray slipped out of his grip, and the glasses smashed all over the floor.

''Aw, shit!'' Jimmy said, completely humiliated by his uncle's performance. He wished with all his heart that Joe could somehow just vanish. But as he bent to pick up the shattered glass, Joe was right there next to him, trying to be helpful.

"Leave it!" Jimmy urged him.

But Joe couldn't leave it. He was mortified that he'd broken the glasses, and now he would do what he could to repair the damage.

"It's okay, Joe!" Jimmy yanked Joe's arm away. "Leave it!"

Joe's mouth dropped slightly open. He glanced from Jimmy to the pieces of glass scattered in front of them. Then he stared at Jimmy again, almost as if he wanted to be certain this was the Jimmy Bell he knew from Cortez, Florida. As he stood up, he slowly seemed to come to an important realization. "Listen, excuse me," he said to no one in particular. Then he turned and headed quickly for the door.

As badly as Jimmy wanted to see him leave, he couldn't let him go like that, without saying good-bye. Without at least attempting to smooth things over between them. Joe's presence at the gallery was more than he was prepared to handle. It would take too much effort to find some common ground between his past and present. He was already juggling too many balls. But he loved Joe, and he didn't want to hurt him.

So he hurried outside after him, yelling, "Joe, wait up!"

A throng of newly arriving guests stared at him as he rushed past to catch up with Joe.

"Listen, I'm gonna head out," Joe said, scuffing his shoe against the curb. "I'm starving. I think I'll find a McDonald's. You go in. I'll talk to you a little later."

They wouldn't talk later. They both knew that Joe would go straight to LaGuardia. He'd be on the next available flight to Tampa. Jimmy couldn't think of anything to say that would make either one of them feel better about what had happened.

Casting about for a good excuse, he said, "It's . . . this is work, you know, and . . ." He shook his head. The words sounded lame, even to him.

But Joe, generous as always, pretended to be convinced. "Sure, I get it. Go ahead, dazzle 'em." He permitted himself a hug, as if he needed to have that physical contact to take back home with him. "I'm proud of you, James," he said, taking note of Jimmy's new, adult identity as an artist. "I always have been." Then he turned and with a backwards wave trudged down the street.

A hard lump seemed to have lodged itself in Jimmy's throat as he retraced his steps toward the gallery. He felt bereft, as if he'd lost his dearest friend. Yet it made good sense for Joe to leave. He didn't belong here. He couldn't share this piece of Jimmy's life with him. Jimmy hadn't asked him to go. Joe had come to that decision on his own. It was the correct decision. At the moment, however, that awareness was small comfort.

"Chub!" Joe shouted.

Jimmy turned around.

From halfway down the block, Joe yelled, "See if they know how to smoke a swordfish."

The rest of the evening passed in a haze of champagne and tequila. Jimmy accepted as many glasses as were handed to him. He lost track after the third or fourth, but he couldn't seem to get drunk, much as he might have wanted to blot out his feelings. The party swirled about him in successive waves of laughter and conversation. He heard snatches of compliments thrown his way, fragments of praise, tributes to his talents. People tried to draw him into their groups, but he couldn't stand still long enough to fix his attention on what they were saying. He kept circling the room, smiling and nodding as if their words and presence meant something to him. But all he cared about was seeing Estella.

The crowd had thinned out considerably when Erica and Owen found him at the bar, ordering another tequila.

"Congratulations," Erica said.

Owen flashed him a broad grin. "You found the dog."

Bewildered, he asked, "What?"

"They're all sold. Every painting. They

bought every bloody one!'' Erica triumphantly declared.

"Really? All sold out?"

"You're a smash, darling," she assured him. "Come on, darling, get your things."

He could hear her speaking, but he'd lost the thread of her thought because he'd spotted Estella, standing outside with her back to him, clearly visible through the window. His face exploded into a smile. He stepped forward, then stopped as she turned to face him. He'd imagined her. The woman he was looking at, except that she had blond hair and was about the same height, didn't resemble Estella at all.

It hit him now that she wasn't coming. He grabbed a bottle of tequila from the bar.

As he brushed past Erica, she said, "Let's go downtown and celebrate properly." Then, seeing him move toward the door, she called, "Where are you going?"

"Start without me!" he said, and then he was gone.

A light snow was falling, the first snow Jimmy had ever seen outside of the movies. The sidewalk beneath his feet was slick and icy, and a hard wind was blowing as he walked uptown. At Fifty-ninth Street, instead of turning straight up Fifth Avenue, he decided to take a detour through Central Park. He didn't stop to think that he was courting danger by venturing into the dark, deserted park at this late hour. The liquor had fueled his courage. He felt invincible, like Superman, invulnerable to everything except for one thing that could bring him to his knees. For Superman, it was kryptonite; for himself, it was the absence in his life of Estella.

The clouds had completely obscured the stars, which were hardly visible even on the clearest night because of the city's bright lights. But he had a veteran sailor's uncanny ability to navigate with whatever few, familiar markers he could locate. He stuck to the park drive, using the headlights of the passing cars to help him find the angel at Bethesda Fountain. From there, it took him only a few minutes to reach the Bow Bridge, where he and Estella had met so that she could tell him that Walter Plane had proposed.

He stood alone in the middle of the snow-dusted bridge and gazed up at the sky. Though he would not have described himself as a religious person, he liked to believe that some force greater than himself ordered the affairs of the universe. He trembled, not with fear, though most people would have said that venturing alone into Central Park after dark was reason enough to be fearful. Nor was it the cold that made him tremble, although the temperature was dropping as the intensity of the freakish, early-season storm increased.

The tumultuous events of the past evening

had left him feeling exposed and unmoored. He'd never before stopped to think, *What next?* Circumstances had swept him along. His parents' accidental deaths, Mrs. Dinsmoor's invitations, the job on Joe's boat, Ragno's offer of an art show. Now, he found himself wondering how to connect the dots that formed the design of his life, if indeed there was a discernible pattern imposed by whatever higher power was watching over him.

Perhaps, he thought, the lesson was that no one ever knew what came next. So maybe the best a person could do was to chase his dreams and seize his destiny. He tipped the bottle of tequila to his mouth and made a silent toast, *To us, Estella.* When the red-hot glow of the alcohol hit his stomach, he crossed the bridge and headed for Mrs. Dinsmoor's brownstone.

The house was completely dark. Not a single light was visible behind the heavily curtained windows. He unlatched the wrought-iron gate in front of the house, climbed the stairs, and rang the bell.

The house remained silent. He rang the bell a second time. When he still got no response, he began beating on the door with his fists.

"Let me in!" he screamed. "Let me in! I did it! I'm a wild success! I sold them all, all my paintings. You don't have to be embarrassed by me anymore. I'm rich. Isn't that what you wanted? Isn't that great? We're finally happy! All these years, don't you understand?''

At the house across the street, a window flew open. A light went on next door to Mrs. Dinsmoor's. This was not a neighborhood that was used to loud voices or late-night disturbances. People were curious. They wanted to know what was going on. They wanted the racket to end as quickly as it had begun.

Jimmy wanted Estella. Nothing and no one was going to stop him until she opened the door and invited him in. She had to be home. He needed her to be there, tonight of all nights. And in case she hadn't yet gotten the picture, he would draw her a diagram. He took one last swig of tequila, turned the bottle over, and carefully splashed the alcohol across the stoop of the house.

''Everything I've ever done has been for you, anything that might be special in me is you!'' he bellowed. ''Everything that might be good is you!''

He pulled out his cigarette lighter, flicked it on, and dropped it to the ground. The spilled tequila burst into flames. The blaze took shape—a heart on fire in the middle of Manhattan.

What his words could not accomplish, his fiery valentine did. The lock on the door buzzed, signalling him to enter. Jimmy turned the knob and walked into the brownstone.

He blinked his eyes as he adjusted to the darkness that was blacker than the night. Eventually, he was able to make out a winding staircase that curved toward a crack of pale yellow light on the second floor. With one hand on the bannister to guide himself, he hurried up the stairs. The light was coming from beneath a closed door at the top of the landing.

His heart was pounding. He took a deep breath to steady himself. Estella's name was on his lips as he pushed the door open.

"What a lovely surprise," Mrs. Dinsmoor said.

She was lying on her bed, stroking her dead cat.

He was too shocked to speak. She smiled and patiently waited for him to recover. Finally, he mustered enough presence of mind to ask her, "What are you doing here?"

"In this house?" She laughed gaily, as if he'd just told her the most wonderful joke. "I own it. I was born here. Haven't been here in ages, but—"

"Where's Estella?"

"But since I had to come up for the big event," she continued, ignoring his interruption, "I figured why not stay in the old place? Tabby loves it. Don't you, sweet boy?"

"Big event?" He peered around the bedroom, expecting to find Estella hiding in one of the corners as she would have done in the old days at Paradiso Perduto. "My opening?"

"Now, now," Mrs. Dinsmoor scolded. "You enjoyed it. Don't fuss so. And I warned you years ago. I didn't have to do that. I said, 'She'll hurt you terribly.' Didn't I? You chose not to listen. Well, I suggest you look at the bright side. We are together. Joined. You, Estella, and I. A pyramid of pain. It's not love, but it is a bond. We are together."

He'd always known she was cruel, and he'd long ago figured out she was crazy. But now he saw that her madness had completely taken her over, had infected her to the depths of her soul, stifled the last surviving vestiges of decency. She had cultivated and nurtured her grief, allowing it to grow as wild as the jungle vegetation that surrounded her mansion. There was no room left for even the most delicate strands of compassion or human kindness.

He'd made no attempt to hide his heartache from her. But all she could do was crow over his anguish, exult in the fact that she'd accurately predicted his misery. She seemed almost excited by his torment as she lay on her bed, smiling from behind her grotesque mask.

He was tempted to leave. But he couldn't, not without one final effort to make her feel his pain. He would be satisfied with even the smallest sign that she was aware of the damage she'd perpetrated against him and Estella.

"Give me your hand," he said.

Flustered by his demand, she hesitated. She was accustomed to giving orders, not receiving them. Perhaps it was the gleam of determination in his eye that made her do as he'd asked. She raised her arm. Jimmy took her hand, which felt like the most fragile, withered autumn leaf, and placed it on his left breast.

"What is this?" he asked her.

Her lips quivered. He knew she was remembering the day she'd asked him the very same question. "Your..." Her voice trailed off, and she shook her head. She wanted him to stop, to leave her alone. She didn't want to believe that anyone else could suffer as she had suffered.

But he needed her to know that the bond she'd worked so hard to create, the "pyramid of pain" that would forever link him to her and Estella, had crushed a part of him that might never be repaired.

"My heart," he whispered. "My heart is broken. Can you feel it? You did that to me." He held her hand over his heart, and his eyes locked with hers. He didn't let go until he saw the glint of tears that she refused to shed.

"I'm sorry," she whimpered.

Her apology had come too late. He turned and left without acknowledging it. A horrible wail pursued him as he walked down the marble stairs.

"I'm sorry!" she shrieked.

He glanced back. She stood at the top of the stairs, a pale, thin wraith. ''What have I done?'' she cried out, wringing her hands.

She would have to find her own answers. It was too late for him to help her. He wasn't even sure he could help himself anymore.

Barefoot and dressed only in her nightgown, she followed him outside. He could hear her shouting his name, as if she were searching for him. ''Jimmy? Jimmy?''

He kept walking. He refused to reach out to her. And because he didn't turn back, he missed seeing her standing alone in the snow, tears streaming down her face. She spun round and round, a top gone out of control, a child searching for her parent, a crazy old lady lost in her madness, too far gone for redemption.

A jet roared overhead. The plane streaked through the sky, glimmering like a shooting star above the city. Jimmy wondered who the passengers were and where they were going. He envied them, making their escape. Perhaps one of them was feeling as he was, dejected and heartsick, unlucky in love. He raised his arm and saluted the travelers, wishing them a safe journey.

He couldn't have guessed that the jet was carrying only two passengers, and that he knew them both. One was Walter Plane, who'd been on the phone with Japan, negotiating a deal, even before the jet had left the runway. The other was Estella. She was leaning forward in her seat, her face pressed against the window. She was staring down at the city, straining to catch a glimpse of a familiar landmark, wondering why the choices she made only seemed to bring her sadness.

CHAPTER 10

It should have been the happiest night of Jimmy's life. It was turning out to be the worst and the longest. But he'd made a new friend—Rafael, the kid who'd picked him out as an easy mark until he'd sneaked up and tried to mug Jimmy on the pier overlooking the East River.

"Don't you wonder how different your life would have been if just one thing, one little thing, hadn't happened?" Jimmy had asked Rafael, after he'd swatted the kid upside the head, grabbed his gun, and insisted that they have a drink together.

"All the damn time," Rafael had agreed, rubbing the sore spot on his cheekbone where Jimmy had slammed him with a bottle of rum.

Anesthetized by the alcohol, they'd settled into a companionable silence while they finished off the rest of the rum. They watched the snow fall on the river until their feet and hands were numb with cold. Only then was Jimmy ready to go home. He wordlessly returned the gold necklace he'd taken from Rafael and shook his hand. He hoped the kid had learned a lesson. He'd learned a hard lesson himself tonight, one that had been a long time coming.

The streets of TriBeCa were deserted at this early morning hour, halfway between darkness and dawn. His weariness felt like an anchor around his neck, dragging him down into sleep. At the end of the block, he saw an old man scurrying in his direction. The old man, his long gray hair flapping in the wind, stopped to consult a scrap of paper that he'd pulled out of a small canvas bag, then scuttled around the corner, out of Jimmy's sight.

A moment later, a trio of thugs materialized on the otherwise empty street. They glared at him as they swaggered toward him. If they were trying to scare him, they would have to work harder. Nothing they might pull could make him feel worse than he already did.

They surrounded him, gave him the once-over. *Screw you, jerks,* he thought, and stalked past them. He could hear them behind him as he got closer to his building. He quickened his pace and pulled out his keys. He was bone-tired, not in the mood to do battle. He needed his bed. He needed sleep. But if they wanted to fight, he was ready.

He slipped inside his building and slammed the door. The goons must have lost interest in him, because the door stayed closed. He yawned and almost fell asleep standing up as the elevator creakily rose to his floor. He unlocked his door and was about to step inside when he thought he heard somebody say, "Pst!" He looked around, saw no one, decided he was imagining things. But there it was again: "Hey! Hello?"

He traced the voice to the bottom of the stairwell. The old man he'd noticed earlier on the street was huddled against the wall. The man saw Jimmy staring down at him and stepped forward. "I'm in trouble," he said, so quietly that Jimmy had to strain to catch his words. "Some guys are after me. Can I use your phone? I know it's weird, but if I could just use your phone to call the police? Please?"

The man looked too frail to cause any problems, and Jimmy believed his story because he'd seen the goons himself. He couldn't turn away some harmless old geezer. "Sure, come on up," he said, making up his mind to throw the man out as soon as the police arrived.

"Thanks," the man said, starting up the stairs. "I'm sorry," he wheezed, as he reached Jimmy's fourth-floor landing. "It's a . . . situation. Only take a second."

Jimmy opened the door. "Over here," he said, and pointed to the phone. He needed something to drink, he suddenly realized, and plain old water wasn't going to quench his thirst. Tequila, he decided, and reached into the cupboard for a bottle.

The old man, meanwhile, had shed his coat and dialed 911. "Hello?" He spoke urgently into the receiver. "Yes, I'm in trouble. Some people are following me. If you could send a police car to—" He turned to Jimmy. "What's the address?"

Jimmy poured himself a shot of tequila. "One eleven Prince," he said.

"One eleven Prince," the old man repeated. He nodded. "Yes, as soon as possible. Thanks." He hung up and joined Jimmy at the counter.

Okay, Jimmy thought. He'd done his good deed for the day.

The old man said his name was Lustig, and he seemed more interested in the loft than in talking about his pursuers. He glanced admiringly around the space, noticing the easel and paint, the paintings leaning against the walls. "This your place? You an artist?"

Jimmy nodded. "In fact, my show opened tonight."

Lustig stroked his beard. "Yeah. What's your name?"

"James Bell." Jimmy yawned again.

"James Bell." Lustig smiled, and then he said, "Jimmy."

Something about Lustig's tone—the way he'd spoken Jimmy's nickname, as if they were old friends—made Jimmy focus more closely on his face, what he could see of it beneath the beard. Lustig looked as if he'd spent a lot of time outdoors. His skin was rough and weatherbeaten. Deep grooves were etched on either side of his mouth. His eyes were dark and brooding.

"Do I know you?" he asked.

Lustig appeared to be amused. "You don't recognize me?"

Jimmy shook his head. "No."

Lustig put down his glass and took a couple of steps so that now he was standing directly in front of Jimmy. He grabbed his arm with one hand and clapped the other across Jimmy's mouth.

"I know your name," he whispered.

Jimmy's eyes widened as the words catapulted him back to an island in DeSoto Bay, to the most terrifying event of his life. The memory came back to him now. The voice was the same, even if the face had changed as the convict had aged.

"That's right, my boy," Lustig said. "Look at you." He wrapped his arms around him and smothered him in a hug.

Jimmy recoiled from him in horror. Was it

bizarre coincidence that had thrown him together with Lustig after so much time had
passed or had the convict deliberately tracked
him down? What did he want from him? Why
was he here? The terror of that long-forgotten
experience engulfed him with the inexorable
force of a floodtide overflowing its banks. He
pulled himself free of Lustig's grasp and re-
examined his features, finding in them now a
resemblance to the convict who'd threatened
his life.

He felt the years collapsing on him as Lustig
clapped his hands with delight. "I know," he
said. "You're probably wondering what happened to me."

The alcohol made him honest. "Not really,"
he said, wishing he could close his eyes and
make Lustig disappear.

Lustig either didn't hear his answer or chose
to ignore it. Intent on providing an explanation,
he said, "I escaped. After I saw you, I escaped
again. I relocated. Been living abroad. Until
now." He picked up his glass, sipped the tequila, smiled joyously. His eyes gleamed as he
drank in Jimmy's presence. "Jimmy, I've been
looking forward to this for a long time."

His naked, undisguised pleasure only served
to escalate Jimmy's sense of panic and dread.
He was ten years old again, scared and de-
fenseless, facing a younger, much more frightening version of this helpless old man who

seemed so pleased to be remaking his acquaintance. He stared out the window, waiting for the moment to pass, for Lustig to be gone.

After what felt like an interminable pause, Jimmy cleared his throat. "Well," he said. "I'm glad you came by . . ."

He turned around and was shocked to find Lustig wiping his sleeve across his eyes, as if he were blotting up tears.

"So who's this handsome young fellow?" Lustig said, walking over to examine a portrait of his younger self. "Looks like you thought a little about me, too."

"How could I forget? You scared the shit out of me," Jimmy said. Yet he'd chosen not to show this painting but rather a more recent version, because Erica had told him the face seemed too sympathetic, not sufficiently intimidating.

Deaf to the anger in Jimmy's voice, Lustig chuckled. "I like it. How much? I mean, is it for sale?"

"Sorry, it's sold. Actually, my whole show sold out."

Lustig lifted his glass and toasted him again. "Congratulations."

"I've been lucky," Jimmy said shortly. He was desperate now for Lustig to leave. He felt unsafe with him in the loft, not because Lustig posed a physical threat, but because his manner felt too comfortable, too intimate, as if he belonged here with Jimmy.

"No," Lustig contradicted him. "You deserve your success. You're a talented man. Quite a talent." He helped himself to another shot of tequila and slowly walked from one end of the room to the other as he sipped his drink. "And this is quite a place. Might a guy like me be personal enough to ask you what it costs?"

"The rent?" Jimmy sank down on the couch. "I don't know. It's taken care of."

Lustig grinned. "Really? By whom?"

Jimmy was tempted to tell him it was none of his business who paid the goddamn rent. He was also tempted to grab a pencil and start sketching Lustig as he looked today—a companion piece to his portrait of the convict as a young man. His face had so much character, so many interesting lines and shadows. And that beard . . .

He stifled the impulse and said, "A lawyer. Why?"

Lustig shrugged. He pulled up a chair and sat down as if he were settling in for a long visit. "No reason. Just glad to see things working out for you." He beamed at Jimmy, like a proud parent reunited with his beloved son after a long separation.

The image of Joe bending to pick up the pieces of broken glass flashed through Jimmy's mind. It should have been Joe, not Lustig, sitting here with him now. But Joe was on his way back to Florida, and Lustig was making Jimmy feel more uneasy with each passing moment. "I'm sure the cops will be here any minute," he said pointedly.

Lustig winked, letting him in on a private joke. "I didn't call 'em," he said.

But Jimmy had heard him speaking to the 911 operator . . . or so Lustig had led him to believe. "Why not?" he asked, almost dreading to hear the answer.

"Can't," Lustig said calmly. "They're after me."

"What about those guys downstairs?" Jimmy asked apprehensively.

Lustig dismissed them with a wave of his hand. "Old associates of mine. They got some problems they should've gotten over a long time ago."

"I really think you should be going now," Jimmy said, in what he hoped was a menacing tone. He'd saved Lustig's life once already. How many more times would he have to bail him out of trouble? Wasn't there a statute of limitations on this sort of thing?

"Just give me a minute," Lustig said, smiling. "It was good to see you, Jimmy—a grown-up. A man now. Up here, mixing with these people, living this life. My Jimmy, a famous artist. Congratulations on all your suc-

cess, your show, everything. Here's to you."
He raised his glass and knocked back the last
of the tequila.

"I appreciate that, I really do. But right now
you're making me really uncomfortable, and I
think you should go," Jimmy said firmly. He
stood up and took a couple of steps toward the
door.

"Okay." Lustig nodded agreeably as he un-
zipped his canvas bag. He dug around in the
bag until he found what he was looking for—a
semi-automatic pistol, which he casually stuck
in his waistband. He said, "I don't want you
to feel badly."

"Maybe if it was another day, we could go
out for a drink or something," Jimmy said, trying not to stare at the gun.

Lustig buttoned his suit jacket and put on
his coat. "I just came to say hello to you and
see how you're doing. Now I'm happy. This is
great. This is how it should be." He gave
Jimmy a friendly thump on the back and
reached for the door. "Ragno did a good job,"
he said.

It took the span of a heartbeat for Jimmy to
begin to grasp the implications of Lustig's
parting words. "Wait!" he yelled and rushed
out after him. "Don't go! I saw them when I
came in. They're out there, three of them."

The elevator had just reached the fourth
floor. "I know," Lustig said, as the door

opened. "I'll be okay. I'll do what I do."

No way he was going to let Lustig walk into that trap. "Come on," he said. He grabbed Lustig's arm and pulled him toward the window in the hall at the rear of the building. The goons were probably waiting for Lustig to come out the front door. He didn't have to make their lives easy by doing the expected. Even with the gun, three against one were not great odds.

The questions would come later. There was no time to talk now. Jimmy pushed open the window and stepped out onto the fire escape. He peered down at the yard but saw no sign of anyone lurking there. He motioned to Lustig to follow him. They scrambled down the fire escape until they reached the second-story platform. Jimmy lowered the short steel ladder that was bolted to the platform and jumped the final ten feet to the ground. He rolled out of the way and watched uneasily as Lustig got ready to come after him.

Lustig tossed down his canvas bag and leaped after it. He landed awkwardly on his side. Jimmy reached out to help him up, but Lustig shook him off and pulled himself to his feet. Jimmy sidled around the corner of the building until he caught a glimpse of the thugs hanging out in front of the building, waiting for Lustig. He quickly rejoined Lustig and directed him through a concrete tunnel that abutted the backyard. They came out the other end onto an empty street.

There wasn't a taxi in sight, but the entrance to the Chambers Street subway station was only two blocks away. Jimmy figured that if Lustig hopped on a train before the thugs found him, he could find his way to safety somewhere outside the city. He led Lustig at a brisk pace toward the subway, glancing warily around to make sure the thugs weren't following them.

When the lit green bulb of the subway station came into view, he finally allowed himself to ask, "So you know Ragno?"

Lustig nodded, trying to catch his breath. "Good man . . . for a lawyer."

Jimmy digested his comment as they descended into the station, purchased tokens, and hustled through the maze of tunnels that led to the tracks. It felt like a lot to absorb in not very much time. He struggled to fit together the pieces of the puzzle that had been his life for the past several months. Lustig knew Ragno. Ragno must have told him where Jimmy lived. Ragno wouldn't have given out that information to just anyone. The conclusion was disturbing but unavoidable.

Three men and a woman were already waiting for the uptown express. Jimmy scanned the downtown platform on the other side of the tracks but didn't recognize any of Lustig's would-be assailants among the handful of people standing on the platform.

"Look, I'm trying to understand," he said, beginning to feel more secure now that it seemed as if they'd lost the thugs. "You did all this? Brought me up here? Everything?"

A smile crossed Lustig's lined face. "That's right."

Jimmy was about to ask him the most important question—why?—when he spotted the hit men on the downtown platform across the four sets of tracks. "Shit!" he said.

Lustig followed his gaze and scowled. He unbuttoned his coat so that his gun was partly visible, but he didn't say anything. If he had a plan in mind, he was keeping it to himself.

The thugs walked right up to the edge of the platform. "Hey, Arthur," one of them shouted across the tracks. "Whatta ya doin'?"

Lustig's eyes darted right, then left, as he checked out the people milling about him. Jimmy thought about all the years he'd spent on the lam, how practiced he must have become at watching his back and avoiding surprises. So how had these guys caught up with him? Was it because he'd gone sentimental and opted for a reunion with a kid he'd met only once on a beach?

"Waitin' for the train. You?" Lustig yelled back.

"You look like Howard Hughes," the thug

taunted him. "You been on a desert island all these years?"

Lustig's only response was a brief shrug. Jimmy looked down the track, hoping to see the lights of an approaching train. No such luck. Nothing was coming.

"Come on. Tommy doesn't want any trouble. He just needs to talk," the thug urged Lustig.

"I know," Lustig shouted. "Gimme his number. I'll call him."

The thug pointed to the stairs. "Arthur, he's upstairs."

"I'm down here," Lustig said. "That's life."

"We'll work this thing out," the thug promised him. "I'm comin' over, Arthur. You wait."

Lustig nodded, and for a moment Jimmy thought he actually planned to stick around. But as soon as the three goons had disappeared up the stairs, Lustig grabbed his arm. "Let's go," he said and sprinted toward their set of stairs.

They could hear footsteps coming in the opposite direction when they reached the upper platform. Lustig pulled Jimmy behind an enormous column that bisected the platform just in time to avoid being seen by the thugs who raced past them. They huddled there until the trio disappeared down the far stairs.

Then it was back across the platform and down another set of stairs to the express side of the station. Only one set of tracks separated them now from the goons—and one of them had disappeared.

"I thought you guys wanna talk," Lustig called to them. He peered around, searching for the missing man. "You lose Victor?"

Jimmy's prayers were answered as the express train finally barreled into sight. The goons looked at each other, trying to decide what to do. The train was moving too fast for them to run up the stairs and cross the platform to the express side. The distance across the tracks was too far for them to jump. Frozen with indecision, they watched the train pull into the station.

The doors opened on Jimmy's and Lustig's side of the platform. They boarded an empty car and breathed sighs of relief as the goons took out their frustration by banging on the shatterproof glass of the closed metal doors.

Home free! The train pulled out of the station, and Lustig grinned at Jimmy. "Bet you don't have this kind of fun with your artist pals."

Jimmy managed a weak smile. Lustig almost seemed to be enjoying himself, but it was only a lucky break that the train had arrived when it did. "We'll change at Canal," he said, hurriedly formulating an escape route. "Get the express to Kennedy. After that, you're on your own.''

Lustig patted him on the shoulder. "You'll miss me."

"I guess," he said.

Lustig winked at him. "Take the train to the plane," he sang in an off-key, monotonous tone. "Take the train to the plane."

Jimmy smiled tiredly. He still didn't have an answer to why Lustig had plucked him out of Florida and bankrolled his artistic career. But it was a long trip out to Kennedy. He'd have plenty of time to find out what he needed to know.

The train rattled on. The lights flickered, dimmed, then died altogether. The car went dark, except for the occasional streak of light from the tunnel. Jimmy's eyes felt heavy, and the urge to doze off was too strong to resist. His head fell to one side as he slid into sleep. Some moments later, a loud hissing noise startled him awake. Someone had pushed open the door to their car.

He blinked his eyes, straining to see through the shadowy gloom. He just barely made out a large, hulking figure moving toward him and Lustig. Before he had a chance to move or warn Lustig, the intruder lunged at Lustig and threw three short jabs into his chest.

The lights flashed back on. Lustig was slumped down onto the seat next to Jimmy. His assailant, the thug who'd earlier called him by name, dashed to the far end of the car and disappeared through the connecting door.

Jimmy jumped up and started after him. But his foot slipped on a wet spot, and he almost fell. He looked down and found himself standing in a widening pool of blood. Lustig was holding his hand over his heart. Streams of blood were pumping through his fingers. He stared at Jimmy, a look of profound shock in his eyes.

Jimmy lunged for the emergency brake, but Lustig grabbed his arm with unexpected strength before he could reach it. "Don't!" he cried hoarsely. "Don't! Just . . . sit down. Sit here."

He tugged Jimmy down onto the seat next to him and balled his fist over the knife wound. "I'm okay," he muttered.

"No, you're not. You're hurt bad," Jimmy said, close to tears. Lustig's shirt was stained bright red. He needed to get help. He needed to stop the train and find the conductor.

"I'll outlive you. Sit down," Lustig whispered.

Jimmy reluctantly obeyed him. He was afraid that if he left Lustig, even for a second, something too terrible to contemplate would happen.

"Good," Lustig said. "Good boy."

The train clattered its way uptown. Jimmy

tried to calculate how many more minutes until they'd reach Canal Street, the next stop. He would hold the doors open there, scream for help. They'd call an ambulance and get Lustig to the nearest hospital. He couldn't be hurt that badly. He'd be okay if only the bleeding would stop.

Lustig tilted his head back against the hard plastic seat and gripped Jimmy's hand with his own blood-streaked free hand.

"I never made much," he murmured. "You know, bullshit money. But whatever I made was for you. It all went to you."

Jimmy stared at him, willing him to live. He wanted to tell him to be quiet, to save his strength. But he sensed that Lustig needed to talk, and he wanted to hear his story.

Lustig's face was pale and ashen. A pulse beat weakly in his forehead. He said, "Sometimes I'd be sitting in a room in some hotel on the other side of the world. Alone. I'd see you. Your face back then. Little kid out there in that fucked-up boat." He chuckled weakly, and the laugh turned into a cough. He looked down at his blood-covered chest and said, "Jesus, what a mess."

He pulled his jacket closed to cover the stains. "I did bad things in my life," he said, as the blood seeped through his coat. "Whatever I had to do. But you . . . My one good thing."

Blood was dripping off the seat now, soaking a newspaper that lay crumpled on the floor. Jimmy had never seen so much blood.

"Your show," Lustig mumbled. "I bought it. For you."

Lustig was speaking so faintly that Jimmy thought he might have misheard him. Each word seemed like a tremendous effort for the old man. Jimmy leaned in closer as Lustig said, "I bought 'em. All of 'em. The whole goddamn show."

"You bought all my paintings?" Of all the things Lustig had told him tonight, he felt most shocked by this revelation. Erica had assigned a high price to each of the portraits. Lustig would have had to spend a fortune to buy the entire collection. But Jimmy believed him. He was too close to death to be telling anything less than the truth.

Lustig winced with pain as he reached into his coat and pulled out a blood-streaked envelope. "Open it," he told Jimmy.

Jimmy pulled out a faded piece of paper and unfolded it. He almost wept when he found himself looking at the pencil drawing of a barracuda, a picture drawn by a ten-year-old boy. The faded page turned brown with age, was stained with Lustig's bloodied fingerprints.

"I love the way you draw. Always have," Lustig whispered. "What's the time?"

"Almost six," Jimmy said, stunned to realize that Lustig had carried the drawing with him all these years.

"Okay, good." He leaned back against the seat and sighed. "We're all right."

Jimmy moved closer to Lustig and draped his arm around his shoulder. Cradling the old man as gently as if he were a tired child on the edge of sleep, he shifted his position until Lustig's head came to rest on Jimmy's shoulder. As the train rumbled through the darkness, Lustig closed his eyes. He uttered a long, throaty sigh that seemed to come from the very deepest part of his being, and then his head fell slack.

After some time, Jimmy realized that he could no longer feel the old man's breath on his neck. Lustig had engineered his final escape. But he had found a measure of peace in his turbulent life. A little boy had given him a shot at freedom, and he had dreamed that he might eventually return that favor. He had died with a smile on his lips because he had lived to see his dream fulfilled. As Jimmy's tears fell on the old man's face, he could only pray that someday he might say the same for himself.

CHAPTER 11

Coming home was so much easier than Jimmy could have imagined. After seven years, it felt so natural to be back in Cortez, back in the same apartment he'd lived in as a child. Only now did he realize that he'd stayed away too long, for reasons he didn't understand and had never stopped to analyze.

His motive for leaving New York had seemed so simple that morning after Arthur Lustig had died in his arms: he needed to go some place where no one knew his name or anything else about him. He hadn't stopped to consider that he was doing the same thing Lustig had done all his life. "Relocating," Lustig had called it. Put more simply, he'd been running away.

He'd needed the distance, from Lustig's death, from his memories of Estella and Mrs.

Dinsmoor, from the madness of the New York
art scene, from Erica Thrall and Owen Tulp
and Carter MacLeish. Overwhelmed with grief
and confusion, he'd looked at a map of the
world, and Paris had beckoned. His self-
imposed exile had been good for him in many
ways. He'd learned a lot about himself, living
so far away from everything that was familiar
to him, solely dependent on his own resources
to further his career. He'd learned to be a better
artist, maybe even a better person.

Perhaps, more than anything, it was his
sense of shame about how he'd treated Joe on
the night of his opening that had kept him in
France long past the point that he'd established
his reputation as an artist. He might never have
forgiven himself and returned for a visit if it
hadn't been for the birth announcement and
baby picture that arrived one day in the mail.

"Please come see us and meet your name-
sake, baby Jimmy," Diane Rhinebold had written on the back of the announcement. After all
this time, Joe finally had a son of his own.

For Joe's life had changed greatly, and much
for the better, since Jimmy had seen him last.
A year after Jimmy had moved to Paris, Maggie had finally made good on her frequent
threats to leave her long-suffering husband.
She'd run off with a computer salesman from
Miami who'd paid for her to get a divorce in
the Dominican Republic. But how fortunate for

-Joe that Diane had been right there across the street to console him with warm casseroles and a sympathetic ear. Their friendship had gradually ripened into love, and Joe had asked Diane to be his wife.

He would only be compounding his sin, Jimmy decided, if he denied Joe—and himself—the pleasure of seeing the family reunited. So he'd booked a flight to the States and called to tell Joe he was on his way. And here he was, seated at the kitchen table while Diane cleared the dinner dishes and Joe did the washing up. He felt as if he'd left only yesterday.

"Dinner was terrific, Di," he said, dandling his little cousin on his lap.

"Liar," she said agreeably, as she leaned over to kiss her son, whom everyone agreed was the spitting image of Jimmy when he was the same age. She nodded at her husband and grinned. "You do know this performance is for you, Jimmy. Joe hasn't touched a dish in years."

Joe couldn't seem to stop smiling. He winked at Jimmy behind Diane's back.

Diane stacked another pile of dishes next to the sink. "He does help with his son, though," she said. "I'll give him that."

"Yeah. He's a good dad," Jimmy agreed, watching Joe reward Diane with a kiss.

It was as clear as the Florida sky that Diane had brought Joe the happiness he deserved. Her influence was everywhere in the apartment: The walls had finally been painted, the frayed couch and chair in the living room had been replaced, and Joe had even sprung for a new kitchen table. The dinner plates were new, as well, and a great improvement, in Jimmy's opinion, over the plastic dishes he remembered from his childhood.

He was touched to notice that Joe had saved every one of the postcard invitations he'd sent for the various French gallery openings of his exhibits. The refrigerator door was covered with an informal, postcard homage to his work. By sheer coincidence—for he'd never told Joe the story of the escaped convict who'd become his patron saint—a portrait of Lustig, printed on the front of a gallery invitation, had the place of honor at eye level on the door.

He'd painted Lustig's portrait again and again over the years. The man's still face haunted his waking hours as well as his sleep. He'd painted him as the younger man he'd first known, and as the ravaged older man who had died in his arms. Lustig had become his most famous subject, the one the critics deemed most interesting and praiseworthy.

"You know, they got art galleries in this country, too," Joe said. "You could work here. Get to know your cousin."

"I miss it sometimes," Jimmy admitted. "I

miss you two. Three. I miss the ocean. Cuban food.''

The last plate washed and dried, Joe toweled off his hands. He said, ''Nora Dinsmoor finally died.''

''Really?'' He'd been meaning to ask but hadn't found the right moment to introduce the subject. ''When?''

''A while ago.'' Joe reclaimed his son and expertly patted his diaper to check whether it needed changing. ''It took a few weeks to find her in all that mess.''

''What about the place? Her estate?'' Jimmy asked.

Joe shrugged. He didn't know what had happened to the mansion. It had been so many years since he'd seen Nora Dinsmoor that he hadn't thought to ask.

Jimmy left unspoken the question that mattered most to him: What had happened to Estella? Earlier that afternoon, he'd borrowed Joe's boat and taken a ride out to the island where he'd first encountered the convict. He'd stood on the sand and watched the waves lap against the beach. He'd watched a barracuda flash silver as it hovered in the clear blue water before it disappeared into the depths of the bay. He'd thought about the seemingly random nature of the universe and the uncanny ways in which people altered other people's lives.

He hadn't said Estella's name aloud in seven

years, but her presence was still as real to him as if he'd seen her just yesterday. Though he'd searched for her in the streets of Paris, and every other European city to which he'd travelled, their paths had never crossed. He'd seen references to her and Walter Plane from time to time in the English magazines and newspapers that he infrequently read. Plane had lost a great deal of money in the early nineties, but more recently he seemed to have rebounded from his financial mishaps. His marriage to Estella had gone sour. She'd almost gotten engaged to the governor of some western state, but the romance had ended, and since then he'd read nothing more about her.

He'd given up believing that he'd ever get over her. That was too much to hope for. If he was lucky, her memory might one day grow faint enough that he could stop comparing every woman he met to the only woman he ever loved.

A farewell visit to Paradiso Perduto might help him make peace with his memories, and he couldn't go back to Paris without paying his last respects to Mrs. Dinsmoor. So the next morning he drove the car he'd rented at the airport south along the coast to Sarasota. The route was so familiar that he made the turns automatically and didn't once have to consult a map in order to find his way to the estate.

The outer wall that guarded the estate was

still intact, but a steel chain hung across the entrance. He stepped over the chain and walked down the path, which was so thickly overhung with trees that the sky temporarily disappeared above the canopy of green. But the real shock came when he reached the end of the path. Where the mansion had formerly stood, there was now a flat, graded, dirt-covered field. The mansion had been destroyed. The jungle had been levelled. Pink surveyor flags fluttered in the morning breeze. Wooden stakes had been placed at carefully spaced intervals to mark the sites of future homes in what was likely to be yet another west coast Florida retirement community development.

He felt as disoriented as if he'd just been transported to the moon. Paradiso Perduto was gone, and with it a huge chunk of his childhood. He almost wished now that he hadn't come. He would have preferred to remember the place in all its decrepit, tumbledown glory.

He wasn't sure he could stay much longer with so little left to see. But as he considered leaving, a ladybug landed on his wrist, stayed for a moment, then flew away. Or perhaps the ladybug was a figment of his imagination. Perhaps the lure of nostalgia was so strong that he was reliving the moment he'd first met Estella. When he closed his eyes, he could see the mansion looming before him. He could hear a little girl giggling nearby.

He opened his eyes, blinked, and saw that the little girl was no whimsical invention of his brain, but a very real flesh-and-blood creation. She was a young Estella, the same blond hair framing the face he remembered from his fantasies. He stood rooted to the spot, watching as she chased a butterfly through the bushes until she reached the tunnel that led to the beach on the other side of the wall.

When he saw her skip through the entrance of the tunnel, he started after her. He followed her through the darkness toward the glow of light at the other end. It all came back to him now—the ocean breeze, the roar of the waves, Mrs. Dinsmoor dancing on the beach.

Before he could catch up with the little girl, the light was temporarily blocked as a woman—he could tell from the shape of the silhouette—entered the tunnel at the far end. The little girl ran to the woman, whose body was limned in sunlight, and hugged her legs with a breathless laugh. Then she let go and raced off toward the beach. The woman, whose face was obscured by the shadows, moved farther down the tunnel in his direction.

Catching sight of him, she called, ''Can I help you?''

Surely this must be an hallucination, an apparition provoked by his return to the mansion.

Yet he couldn't stop himself from saying her name. "Estella?"

The woman stopped walking. He saw her hand go to her mouth. "Is that you, Jimmy?" she answered, disbelievingly.

"Stay there," he said. "I'll come to you."

As he walked toward her in the darkness, her features began to take on shape. She looked older, of course, the freshness of her beauty vanished with the years. But the beauty had been replaced with something deeper and more real.

She began to laugh, and for a moment he thought she was about to cry. But she stopped herself and said, "How weird. How perfect, huh? To meet here."

"She would have loved it," he said. They both were silent for a moment, thinking of Mrs. Dinsmoor. Then he said, "That little girl, your daughter? Estella, what a beauty."

"I brought her," she said, smiling. "I wanted her to see this place, at least what's left of it. They start building, pouring cement or whatever, tomorrow. I thought I'd take one last visit."

"You don't own it?"

"No. It was sold when I was still married."

There was a hint of pain in her tone that kept him from asking her why she hadn't held onto the property. He remembered Walter Plane's financial problems and wondered whether the estate had gone to bail him out.

"I think of you a lot lately," she said softly. "For a while I didn't. Then, when I understood things . . . life, I guess, better; then I wouldn't let myself. But lately . . . Some things you never forget."

A sad smile crossed her face. He could hear the ocean whispering in the distance, making promises for eternity.

"Some things you don't want to forget," he said.

"Friends?" She held out her hand for him to shake.

"Friends," he said.

By unspoken agreement, they turned and headed toward the beach. There was so much he wanted to ask her, but the questions could wait. He knew that it couldn't have been an accident that had brought him here today of all days. Some things were meant to be. "I speak French now," he said, remembering how she'd mocked him because she knew the language and he didn't.

She nodded, as if she, too, remembered. "Say something," she replied.

He didn't have to stop and think about it. He'd said these words to her in his head a thousand times before. *"Je t'adore,"* he told her.

She slipped her hand into his as they walked out onto the beach, where her daughter was building a sand castle by the water's edge. "Say it again," she whispered.

They were the truest words he'd ever spoken. He would say them as often as she wanted, anywhere, any time. He could see their future taking shape as inevitably as the morning tide washing in to shore. The rich golden yellow sunlight shimmered on the white-capped waves. It was a beautiful picture, more beautiful than anything he could ever hope to paint. For that and so much more, he was infinitely grateful.

Three breathtaking novellas by these acclaimed authors celebrate the warmth of family, the challenges of the frontier and the power of love...

ROSANNE BITTNER
DENISE DOMNING
VIVIAN VAUGHAN

CHERISHED LOVE